TUTANKHAMUN AND THE LUXOR WIDOW

Secrets Carried by the Dead

David Ashe

Tutankhamun and the Luxor Widow

This is a work of fiction. Names, characters, places, and incidents are either the product of the author's imagination or are used fictitiously. Any resemblance to actual persons, living or dead, events, or locales is entirely coincidental.

ISBN (Print Book): 9781937774080
Publisher: Adair Digital Graphics (ADG)
Cover Design: David Ashe
Interior Design: David Ashe

Printed in the United States of America
First Edition, 2026

Dedication

There were no signatures on their work. No names carved into the plaster. No records of their lives beyond the brushstrokes they left behind.

And yet, the artisans of ancient Egypt shaped a world that still breathes.

They painted in cramped chambers lit by lamps. They carved symbols meant to guide a soul through eternity. They carried their tools with reverence, knowing each mark mattered. They worked in teams, in families, in lineages — passing down skill, memory, and devotion.

Their hands are gone. Their voices are gone. But their care remains.

This novella is, in its quiet way, a thank you to them. To the forgotten workers whose labor outlived their names, and whose humanity still reaches us across three thousand years.

Contents

CHAPTER 1: THE ARMOIRE

Abagail found the armoire in the far corner of the attic, half-hidden behind a stack of framed photographs and a box of her grandmother's books. The attic light was weak, filtered through a small window that hadn't been opened in years, and the dust in the air made everything look suspended, as if the room itself were holding its breath.

She ran her fingers over the carved wood, tracing the patterns worn smooth by generations. The brass hinges were dulled, the bottom drawer handle missing, the key long lost. She remembered her mother's stories—how the armoire had traveled from England to Africa, then back again, carrying the family's history in its deep drawers.

Abagail tugged gently at the bottom drawer. It refused to move, swollen from damp and years of neglect. She pressed harder, feeling the wood shift beneath her hands. Something inside shifted—a muted, dense thud against the lining. Not clothes. Not papers. Something older.

She knelt, peering into the gap where the drawer met the frame. The wood was cracked, the seam just wide enough to slip a finger through. She pressed gently. The lining shifted.

"Here," she murmured.

She worked the lining loose, peeling it back just enough to reach inside. Her fingers brushed something smooth, cool, and solid.

She drew it out slowly.

A small leather suitcase, covered in faded travel stickers—Alexandria Port Authority, Cairo Continental Hotel, Luxor Winter Palace, P&O Steamship Line. The leather was cracked, the straps frayed to threads, the metal locks dulled to a soft grey.

Abagail lifted the suitcase carefully, surprised by its weight. Something inside shifted—a muted, dense thud against the lining. Not clothes. Not papers. Something older.

She carried it downstairs.

Emily was in the kitchen, sorting through a stack of envelopes. She looked up when Abagail entered, her expression softening in that way it always did when her daughter appeared with something unexpected.

Abagail set the suitcase on the table. "This was in the armoire. The bottom drawer finally gave way."

Emily came closer. Her breath caught.

She rested her fingers on the lid, the way one might touch a sleeping animal.

The stickers. The leather. The initials.

"I haven't seen this since I was a child," she said quietly. "I thought it was lost."

She ran her fingers over the stickers, tracing the edges of Luxor Winter Palace as if the name might shift under her touch. She didn't say anything more. She didn't need to.

The suitcase looked out of place on the kitchen table—too old, too heavy with its own history. Emily tried one of the locks. It refused. The metal had seized long ago.

"No key?" she asked.

Abagail shook her head.

Emily studied the lock again. The metal was pitted, the mechanism stiff. She pressed her thumb against it, feeling for any give.

Nothing.

She sat down, the suitcase in front of her, and let out a slow breath.

"It's strange," she said. "Your grandmother kept everything in order. But this... she never mentioned it."

Abagail pulled out a chair and sat beside her. "Maybe she forgot about it."

Emily shook her head. "Cherry didn't forget things. Not things like this."

They sat in silence for a moment, the suitcase between them like a question neither of them knew how to ask.

Emily reached for the straps. The leather cracked softly under her touch. She eased one free, then the other.

The locks still refused.

Abagail leaned closer. "Do you want me to get a screwdriver?"

"No," Emily said. "Let's not force it."

She turned the suitcase slightly, examining the hinges, the seams, the way the leather had pulled away from the frame in places. Then she noticed a small tear near the back corner, just wide enough to slip a finger through.

She pressed gently. The lining shifted.

"Here," she murmured.

Together, they worked the lining loose, peeling it back just enough to reach inside. Emily's fingers brushed something smooth, cool, and solid.

She drew it out slowly.

A small alabaster box, wrapped in linen that had yellowed with age.

Abagail stared. "What is that?"

Emily didn't answer. She set the box on the table, her hands steady but her breath not quite.

The linen was soft, worn thin in places. She unwrapped it carefully, revealing the box beneath—pale, translucent, the surface etched with faint scratches that caught the light.

The lid was slightly askew.

Emily touched it with the back of her finger, as if testing whether it was real.

"This wasn't my mother's," she said quietly. "Or Cherry's. This is older."

"How old?" Abagail asked.

Emily didn't look away from the box. "Old enough," she said. "Much older than any of us."

Chapter 2: The Past

The kitchen felt too quiet for the amount of history now sitting on the table. Emily rested her hands on either side of the alabaster box, steadying herself more than the object. Abagail stood close, arms folded, as if unsure whether to touch anything or keep her distance.

They had come to the house to sort through Cherry's things. A month had passed since the funeral, and the rooms still carried her mother's presence — the faint scent of turpentine from the studio, the stacks of contact sheets on the desk, the framed prints leaning against the hallway wall. Emily had avoided the attic until today. She wasn't ready for the last of it. But Abagail had insisted they start somewhere.

Now the suitcase sat open, its contents older than either of them had expected.

Emily reached for the envelope tucked beneath the carved panels. The paper was brittle, the edges softened by time. She turned it over. A name was written on the back in a looping, deliberate hand.

Petal Adair.

Her great grandmother. A woman she knew only from a handful of photographs — a young face in desert light, a linen dress, a man beside her whose name had been lost in the family's quiet.

Emily slid the photographs from the envelope. Glass negative plates followed, wrapped in thin paper.

Abagail leaned closer. "Are those...?"

"Negatives," Emily said softly. "Glass plates. Early twentieth century."

She held one up to the light.

The image was faint but unmistakable — a chamber filled with objects, some upright, some toppled, all crowded together in a way that suggested hurried placement. A lion figurine sat on a folded cloth in the foreground. Behind it, half in shadow, was the alabaster box now sitting on their kitchen table.

Abagail inhaled sharply. "That's the same lion."

Emily didn't answer. She was already studying the angle of the light, the grain of the photograph, the way the shadows fell across the floor. She knew this kind of image — the early documentation style, the long exposures, the careful staging.

She set the plate down carefully and lifted the second.

This one was darker, taken inside a tent. A makeshift darkroom — the kind used by field photographers in the early 1900s. A canvas wall, a wooden table, trays for chemicals. And on the table, arranged with deliberate care, were the same objects now in front of them:

The lion. The alabaster box. The six small panels. The ochre holders. The folded linen.

Abagail whispered, "Mom... this is impossible."

Emily didn't respond. She was tracing the edges of the image with her thumb, noting the faint blur where the photographer's hand must have trembled, the slight overexposure near the lamp.

She recognized the handwriting on the back of the plate — the same looping script from the old family albums. Notes in the margin. A date. A location.

Luxor, Winter, 1922.

She set the photographs aside and turned back to the alabaster box. The lid lay open, the interior lined with folded linen. She lifted the cloth carefully, revealing the six small panels beneath.

They were thin, translucent, carved with symbols:

A lotus. A feather. A reed. A lamp. A lion. A box.

Abagail touched one lightly. “These look like... instructions?”

Emily didn’t answer. She was studying the carvings, the way the symbols were arranged, the faint wear along the edges. She recognized the material — alabaster, the kind used for canopic jars and offering bowls. But these were too small, too deliberate, too specific.

She set the panels aside and reached for the wooden lion. It was warm from her hand, the surface worn smooth. She turned it over, tracing the shallow cuts of the mane.

Then she lifted the ochre holder.

It was small, almost weightless, the wood worn in a way that only comes from years of being turned in the same hand. She rolled it between her fingers, testing the balance the way she did with her own tools. The surface carried a faint residue of red ochre, darkened to a muted rust, caught in the grain like old breath.

There was a shallow indentation along one side — not damage, but the memory of a thumb. She set her own thumb into it, and the fit was immediate, as if the tool had been waiting for a familiar pressure.

The warmth of the wood surprised her. Objects that have been held long enough never quite forget.

Emily shifted her grip on the ochre holder. The weight settled into her palm with a quiet certainty.

The room around her thinned. The air changed — heavier, warmer, touched with dust.

She blinked.

For a moment — only a moment — the room felt misaligned. She was somewhere sunlit and warm, where stone walls held the heat of afternoon and a man worked in silence at a low table.

A courtyard. A strip of shadow. A hand carving a symbol into alabaster.

The image flickered, like a memory she had never lived.

Then it was gone.

The kitchen returned. The table. The box. The lion. The six panels.

Emily set the ochre holder down carefully, her breath unsteady.

"Mom?" Abagail whispered.

Emily didn't answer. She was still listening to the echo of something ancient, something that had waited a long time to be seen.

The past had stirred.

Chapter 3: The Visit

The heat settled first – a dry, steady warmth that softened the edges of the afternoon. Dust drifted lazily in the air, catching the light as it filtered through the reed awning stretched across Menna's courtyard. He sat at his low wooden table, the tools of his craft arranged in a neat semicircle around him.

He worked slowly, not from hesitation but from care. The alabaster panel in his hands was thin and translucent, the surface cool despite the heat. He carved the final line of the lotus symbol with a practiced hand, then held the panel up to the light to check the depth of the cut.

Satisfied, he set it beside the others:

The lotus. The feather. The reed. The lamp. The paints. His son's brushes. The lion. The copper disk. The linen headband. The box.

Six alabaster panels lay together, their symbols distinct, their grouping deliberate.

He reached for the lion next – the small wooden figure his son had carved years ago. The mane lines were crisp, the wood pale and unhandled. He turned it in his palm, checking the balance, the curve of the back, the tilt of the head. A faint smile touched his mouth, the kind that came unbidden when memory rose without warning.

He placed the lion inside the alabaster box beside him. The box was open, empty except for a folded piece of linen – new, unyellowed, its edges crisp. He smoothed the cloth with the back of his hand, then set the lion in the corner, as if settling a child to rest.

A sudden commotion rose from the lane outside — the unmistakable groaning of donkeys, the clatter of tack, the sharp hissing of handlers trying to quiet them. Menna looked up immediately. Visitors at this hour were rare. Visitors on three donkeys were rarer still.

The news itself had come earlier, carried by a palace runner who had reached Set Maat before dawn — swift, breathless, and alone. But the overseer and his escort could not have crossed the cliff paths at such speed. Donkeys were slower, yes, but they were the only animals sure footed enough to carry people and loads across the broken limestone. Gypsum sacks, cedar poles, water jars — all the things a tomb demanded — moved only on their backs.

Nebre, his grandson and apprentice, froze mid stroke over the pigment bowl.

Menna stood and stepped to the doorway.

Three donkeys stood in the dust, stamping and complaining, their necks swaying. Between them, dismounting stiffly, were Panehsy, Overseer of Works for the western necropolis, and a younger priest in travel stained linen. Behind them, a second priest remained mounted, holding a satchel of scrolls.

Menna's breath tightened.

"Panehsy," he said, bowing his head slightly. "This is unexpected."

Panehsy gave a weary nod — a man accustomed to commanding from the high halls above the Valley, where every tomb plan, every corridor angle, every plaster order, and every painting schedule passed beneath his seal. He was the Overseer of all royal tomb works: the cutting, the smoothing, the measuring, the gridding, the pigments, the scaffolds – everything that prepared a tomb before a single brushstroke could be laid.

He did not visit artisans' homes. Ever.

For him to stand in Menna's doorway, dust covered and travel worn, meant the matter was not merely urgent – it was unprecedented.

"Forgive the intrusion, Menna," he said, voice low. "I would not have come myself unless the matter was grave... and unless it required you."

Nebre appeared behind his grandfather, wide eyed. Menna motioned him inside.

"Bring water for our guests," he murmured.

The boy ran.

Panehsy stepped into the courtyard, dust clinging to his sandals. He carried a rolled wooden board under his arm – wrapped in linen, the edges darkened with age. Not a message. Not a summons.

A plan.

"Menna..." Panehsy said quietly. "The king is dead."

The younger priest stepped forward, bowing deeply. His voice was soft, almost reverent. "Tutankhamun has gone west."

The words settled like ash.

Menna closed his eyes for a moment. "When?"

"Last night," the priest said. "His body has been taken to the embalmers. The rites must begin at once. The seventy days will pass quickly."

Menna nodded. Seventy days — the traditional period for purification, drying, anointing, and wrapping. That part was not unusual.

What was unusual was everything else.

The younger priest continued, voice low but urgent. "The overseers fear the tomb will not be ready. They say the king's resting place must be prepared before the final rites. Before the procession. Before the turning of the festival cycle."

Menna exhaled slowly. A tomb — a proper royal tomb — took years. Sometimes decades.

Corridors carved deep into the mountain. Chambers smoothed and plastered. Walls measured, gridded, lined. Scenes drafted, corrected, painted in layers. Pigments ground, mixed, applied. Teams rotating through seasons of heat and flood.

Even the simplest chamber required months of work.

And now they wanted it immediately.

Nebre returned with a clay cup of water. Panehsy accepted it with a nod, then set it aside untouched. His hands were already unwrapping the board.

"I need your eyes on this," he said.

He unrolled the linen. Beneath it lay a charcoal sketch — rough, but unmistakably the outline of a tomb:

the bowl shaped depression
the sixteen steps
the first sealed doorway
the sloping corridor
the second doorway
the antechamber

the burial chamber beyond

Menna leaned over it, tracing the lines with a calloused finger.

"This place..." he murmured. "I remember talk of it. Begun long ago. Abandoned after the first season."

Panehsy nodded. "The upper corridor was cut first. Bad rock. Too many seams. They sealed it and started again lower. That project was abandoned as well. But the lower chambers are sound. Dry. Hidden. Facing west."

Menna tapped the sketch where the corridor angled downward. "The descent is good. The alignment is correct. The mountain embraces it."

The elder priest stepped forward. "Where are your teams now, Master?"

"Scattered," Panehsy answered for him. "Some in the western cliffs above Luxor. Others finishing the tomb of Lady Karestine. A few still in the workshops preparing pigments."

Menna understood the unspoken truth: Everything would have to stop.

Every project. Every commission. Every noble's tomb. Every workshop task.

All of it would be abandoned for the king.

The younger priest added, "The overseers say you must pull your men from every site. Lotus, feather, reed — all of them. They say only you can command them."

Menna's jaw tightened. He had trained these men. He knew their families, their strengths, their tempers. He knew which ones could work in cramped chambers, which ones could paint straight lines on uneven stone, which ones could grind pigment for hours without complaint.

He also knew what he was asking of them.

"They will come," Menna said quietly. "But they must be told why."

The priests exchanged a glance.

"Tell them," Menna said. "Tell them the king needs them. Tell them the valley calls."

He studied the plan again. "There will be debris in the sloping passage. The old corridor above it... its blocking must have failed long ago."

Panehsy gave a grim smile. "You always see what others miss."

Menna didn't answer. His eyes lingered on the burial chamber – small, but workable. A tomb meant for someone of rank, but not a king. A tomb waiting for a purpose.

Panehsy hesitated, then said softly, "Your son would have known this place. He worked on the early cuts."

Nebre's hands stilled.

Menna's jaw tightened. The courtyard seemed to shrink around him.

"We do not speak of that tonight," he said quietly.

Panehsy bowed his head. "Forgive me."

The younger priest cleared his throat gently. "Where shall the workers gather, Master?"

Menna did not need to think.

"In the forecourt of Set Maat," he said. "The workers' village. The staging ground. They know it well."

He looked toward the western cliffs, where the sun was beginning to lower.

Panehsy rolled the plan carefully and placed it in Menna's hands. "The kingdom depends on you."

Menna looked down at the board – at the lines, the angles, the promise of darkness beneath the mountain.

"No," he said softly. "The king depends on us."

Panehsy and the priests bowed, then stepped back into the fading light. The donkeys groaned again as they mounted, their shadows stretching long across the lane.

Menna watched until they disappeared.

Only then did he turn to Nebre.

"Put away the pigments," he said. "Tomorrow you will see a tomb that has slept for years. And you will learn why the mountain remembers everything we do."

Nebre nodded, eyes shining with a mixture of fear and pride.

Menna stood alone in the courtyard, the rolled plan heavy in his hands, the weight of duty – and memory – settling over him like the coming night.

Chapter 4: Set Maat

The village woke before the sun.

A low hum rolled through Set Maat — the sound of grinding stones, clay jars clinking, sandals scuffing across packed earth. Smoke rose from small hearths as women baked the morning bread, the smell of barley and emmer drifting through the narrow lanes. Children ran with water skins, filling jars for the day's work. Donkeys brayed, stamping their hooves, sensing the unusual tension in the air.

Word had spread through the night.

The king was dead. The tomb must be prepared. All hands were needed.

By the time the first light touched the eastern cliffs, the eight team leaders were already in the forecourt, each surrounded by the men of his unit.

The lotus team — plasterers. The feather team — painters. The reed team — draughtsmen. The papyrus team — lamp tenders. The falcon team — scaffold builders. The scarab team — tool sharpeners. The crook team — water carriers. The flail team — donkey handlers and haulers.

Each group moved with purpose, gathering tools, checking loads, tightening rope lashings, filling jars, sharpening chisels. The forecourt looked like a bazar — but one with discipline, hierarchy, and urgency.

Women moved among the men with baskets of warm bread, small bowls of lentils, and jars of thin beer. They pressed food into hands without being asked. Some murmured blessings. Others simply touched a shoulder and moved on.

Menna walked among them, silent, observant.

He saw everything:

the plasterers weighing sacks of gypsum

the scaffold builders sorting cedar poles by length

the lamp apprentices trimming wicks with obsidian knives

the water carriers testing jar seals

the donkey handlers adjusting packsaddles

the women mixing barley mash for the morning meal

Nothing escaped him.

A group of women knelt beside a grinding stone, crushing soft white gypsum into powder. The stone dust rose in pale clouds, settling on their arms and hair. They worked quickly, rhythmically, passing the powder into linen sacks.

Gypsum was the lifeblood of a tomb. Without it, no wall could be smoothed, no surface prepared, no painting begun.

The sacks would be carried on donkeys — the only animals sure footed enough to cross the broken limestone paths. Horses would panic. Camels, even if they had been used in Egypt at the time, would slip and break their legs. Donkeys alone could climb the narrow, twisting paths to thc Valley.

Panehsy arrived shortly after sunrise, his presence commanding immediate stillness. He ducked beneath the awning where Menna and the scribe waited.

"Report," Panehsy said.

Menna gestured to the scribe.

The scribe read from his tablet:

"Gypsum plaster: forty sacks ready, twenty more by midday."

"Cedar poles: twelve full lengths, twenty four half lengths."

"Acacia poles: thirty, cut for corridor turns."

"Rope: sixty cubits of palm fiber, forty of flax."

"Lamp oil: eight jars, more being pressed."

"Wick bundles: forty."

"Water jars: sixty, sealed."

"Donkeys: twelve, loaded."

Panehsy nodded. "And the clearing team?"

"Ready," Menna said. "They leave within the hour."

Under the awning, the leaders gathered around a rough sketch of the tomb layout drawn in chalk on a plank of wood. Menna pointed to the corridor between Door One and Door Two.

"This is the first task. Steps must be cut into the debris slope. A rope line must be fixed. The footing is unstable."

Hapu nodded. "We will send four men ahead — two cutters, one rope man, one lamp carrier."

Kasa added, "And the scribe. He must record the slope angle and debris depth."

Panehsy looked at Menna. "And you?"

"I will follow once the first steps are cut," Menna said. "The mountain must be read as it changes."

Panehsy accepted this with a single nod.

The meeting ended. The leaders dispersed, shouting orders, gathering their teams. The forecourt erupted into motion again — but now with sharper purpose.

Women handed out bread and beer. Men strapped tools to their belts. Donkeys were led forward, their loads balanced and tied. The lamp apprentices carried the alabaster boxes wrapped in linen. The copper disks gleamed in the morning light.

Menna walked through the organized chaos, checking each detail.

"Too much weight on that donkey," he said, adjusting a load. "Those poles must be tied in thirds, not halves." "Trim that wick again — it will smoke." "Fill that jar to the neck, not the rim." "Wrap the copper disk tighter — no scratches."

The men obeyed without hesitation.

By midmorning, the clearing team stood ready at the village gate:

two debris cutters

one rope man

one lamp carrier

the scribe

two guards

Menna inspected them.

"You know the slope," he said. "Cut steps every two cubits. Brace yourselves against the wall. Keep the rope taut. No one moves without the lamp."

The rope man nodded. "We understand."

"Go," Menna said.

They set off toward the Valley, their silhouettes small against the rising cliffs.

Behind them, the full workforce assembled — one hundred thirty men and women, arranged by team, tools in hand, donkeys loaded, water jars sloshing softly.

Panehsy raised his staff.

"Move!"

The caravan surged forward, dust rising beneath their feet. The sound of sandals, hooves, jars, poles, and voices blended into a single living rhythm – the heartbeat of Set Maat.

Menna walked at the front, Nebre beside him, carrying a small bundle of chalk and cord.

"Grandfather," Nebre said quietly, "is this how it always begins?"

Menna looked toward the distant cliffs, where the clearing team was already disappearing into the heat.

"No," he said. "This is how it begins when time is short."

They walked on.

Behind them, the village emptied. Ahead of them, the mountain waited.

Chapter 5: The First Entry

The bowl of rock that held the tomb entrance was even more treacherous in the morning light. Menna stepped down into it carefully, the gravel shifting under his bare feet. The depression sloped inward like a shallow basin, its walls rising sharply on three sides. It was the kind of place where rainwater — rare but violent — would rush and swirl, carrying sand and stones with it.

He crouched and sifted the gravel through his fingers.

"Water has been here," he murmured. "Not recently. But enough to bury the steps."

Hapu nodded. "The storms last season were strong. It could have filled the bowl."

Kasa studied the slope. "Or many seasons. This place may have been open for years."

Menna said nothing, but he agreed. The tomb mouth was not at the bottom of the basin, but cut into the upper inner wall, a few paces up the slope — exactly where runoff would strike hardest. The first three steps were buried. The fourth was half exposed. The fifth caught the morning light like a pale tooth.

He ran his hand along thc cxposed stone. The edges were softened by time, the plaster seal cracked in places — not by looters, but by weather and neglect.

"This tomb has slept a long time," Menna said quietly. "Longer than most remember."

He stood and surveyed the bowl.

"This ground must be cleared. All of it. Down to the threshold."

He pointed to the slope below the entrance.

"And this must be made safe. If the gravel shifts under a man carrying plaster jars or lamp house panels, he will fall."

Hapu tested the slope with his heel. "It will need clearing. And leveling."

Kasa pointed toward the right hand wall. "We can cut footholds there. A path for the men carrying tools."

Menna nodded. "Do it. Before the full teams arrive."

The women moved to the edge of the bowl, marking where the latrine trench would go. The guards took their positions along the rim, watching the approaches.

Menna straightened.

"We go inside first. Before any work begins. Before any clearing. Before any man sets foot here again."

He gestured to the apprentices.

"Light the lamps."

The alabaster light boxes glowed softly in the shade of the bowl. The copper disks caught the light and threw it toward the half buried stairway.

Menna stepped carefully up the slope toward the entrance, testing each foothold, feeling the gravel shift and settle beneath him. At the exposed fourth step, he paused.

"This is where it begins," he said.

He descended the first visible step, the light box held before him.

Behind him, the men held their breath.

The air rising from below was cool and still, touched with the scent of old stone. The steps were dusty but intact. The walls were rough cut limestone, the tool marks still visible — long, shallow grooves where chisels had bitten into the rock. Sand whispered underfoot as the men followed.

At the bottom of the sixteen steps stood the first sealed doorway.

A smooth plastered blocking filled the entire frame, stamped repeatedly with the necropolis seal — a jackal over nine bound captives. The impressions were faint but unmistakable.

Hapu exhaled softly. "This was meant for someone important."

"No," Menna said. "This was meant for someone who never came."

He knelt, running his fingers along the plaster. "Break the upper corner."

Two men lifted a mallet and chisel. They worked carefully, striking only the upper left corner. The plaster cracked, flaked, and finally gave way, revealing a dark void beyond.

A small hole, no more than two feet wide and two and a half feet high.

Menna held the alabaster light box to the opening.

A corridor appeared — long, narrow, filled with construction rubble.

Kasa whispered, “They abandoned it before clearing the debris.”

Menna shook his head. “No. This is not construction rubble. This fell from above.”

Hapu frowned. “From the upper corridor?”

“Yes,” Menna said. “The old passage. Its blocking failed long ago. The debris poured down this slope and stopped at the second door.”

The leaders exchanged glances – not fear, but the quiet recognition of a problem that had to be solved.

Menna stood and turned to the guards. “Bring the rope.”

A coil of palm fiber rope was placed in his hands. He looped it around his waist, tying the knot himself. Two guards braced their feet against the stone, gripping the rope firmly.

Hapu stepped forward. “Master, let one of us go first.”

Menna shook his head. “I must see it with my own eyes.”

He lowered himself through the breach, feet searching for purchase on the debris. The slope shifted under him – soft, unstable, like sand poured into a funnel. He steadied himself with one hand against the wall.

The air was cool. Still. Heavy with the scent of old dust.

“Master?” Hapu called softly.

“I’m here,” Menna answered. “It holds.”

He moved slowly down the slope, the rope taut behind him. The debris filled up about half of the height of the corridor — a mixture of sand, gravel, and small stones. It had poured in over decades, maybe centuries, settling in layers.

Kasa's voice echoed faintly through the breach. "How far does it go?"

Menna lifted the light box, angling it down the corridor.

"Not far," he said. "Door Two is ahead."

The second doorway was half buried — its lower half swallowed by the debris, its upper half exposed. The plaster was cracked but intact. No signs of looting. No tool marks. No footprints.

A sealed chamber. Untouched.

Menna felt a quiet shiver run through him.

He climbed carefully back up the slope, the rope helping him find balance.

Kasa crouched beside the breach, peering into the dim slope of rubble. "Master... is the ceiling sound? The rock above us?"

Menna angled the light box upward, studying the limestone overhead. The ceiling was low, but unbroken — pale layers stacked like pages of a book.

"Yes," he said. "This is good stone. The fissures run higher."

"How much higher?" Kasa asked.

Menna pointed upward, though the men could see nothing but darkness and dust. "The abandoned corridor lies several hundred cubits above this one. Its floor ends almost directly over our heads — that is why the debris fell here and nowhere else."

Kasa nodded slowly. "A weakness in the old passage."

"A weakness in its blocking," Menna corrected. "Not in the mountain. The builders sealed the upper corridor with plaster and stone, but time opened small channels. The debris followed the slope of that passage until it reached this one."

He tapped the ceiling with his knuckles – a dull, solid sound. "But this roof is stable. The layers are thick, the bedding planes tight. The mountain holds."

Kasa exhaled, reassured. "Then the men will be safe."

"They will," Menna said. "Once we clear the slope and brace the entrance. The danger is not the ceiling – it is the footing."

He shifted his weight, and the rubble slid softly beneath him. "This corridor will need steps cut into the debris until we reach the chamber."

Kasa nodded. "We will mark the slope. And the men will count their steps."

Menna gave a faint smile. "Exactly."

When he reached the breach, the leaders pulled him through.

Menna dusted off his hands. "We open Door Two."

Kasa frowned. "Not Door One first?"

Menna shook his head. "If the chamber beyond is sound, we break both doors tomorrow. If it is not... we waste no time."

The leaders nodded. This was the logic of the Valley – always look ahead before committing strength.

Menna gestured to the breach. "Hapu, you come with me. Bring the second light box."

Hapu tied the rope around his waist and slipped through the opening. Together, the two men descended the debris slope again, moving slowly, testing each step.

At Door Two, Menna pressed his ear to the plaster. Nothing. No hollow echo. No shifting stone. The chamber beyond was still.

He tapped the upper left corner. "Here."

Hapu handed him a small chisel.

Menna struck once. Twice. The plaster cracked.

A third strike opened a small hole. Cool air drifted out – dry, untouched, the breath of a sealed room.

Menna lifted the light box and peered through.

A chamber. Empty. Clean. Walls smooth. Rock sound.

He exhaled.

"It will serve," he whispered.

Hapu leaned close. "Master?"

Menna pulled back from the hole. "The chamber is good. The rock is good. The tomb is usable."

Above them, the rope tightened as the guards shifted their stance.

Menna looked up the slope toward the faint glow of daylight. "We return. Tomorrow we clear both doors."

Hapu nodded.

Together, they climbed back toward the entrance, the debris shifting softly beneath their feet.

When Menna emerged into the morning light, the leaders gathered around him.

"Well?" Kasa asked.

Menna wiped dust from his hands. "Tomorrow we prepare the men. The tomb is sound."

A murmur rippled through the group — relief, determination, purpose.

Menna looked toward the valley, its cliffs glowing gold in the rising sun.

"The king will have his house," he said.

And the work began.

The leaders did not leave the tomb. Not yet. The sun was still low, the air cool, and they had hours before the full workforce would arrive.

Menna turned back toward the dark opening. "We go deeper. Today we learn the mountain."

Hapu nodded. "We begin with the corridor."

They widened the breach in Door Two just enough for all eight leaders to pass through. The scribe followed last, tablet tucked under his arm, stylus ready.

Inside the antechamber, the alabaster light boxes cast soft, steady light across the rough walls. The copper disks threw narrow beams that danced across the stone.

Kasa stretched a cord across the west wall. "Seven and a half meters."

Hapu measured the height. "Two and a half at the highest point."

Another leader tapped the floor. "Uneven. We must level it before scaffolding."

Menna nodded. "Mark the low points."

The scribe moved from man to man, capturing every measurement, every observation, every muttered calculation.

They moved into the burial chamber next. The leaders spread out, touching the walls, testing the stone, imagining the work ahead.

"This room will take the longest," Hapu said.

"Not if we sequence it correctly," Menna replied. "The plasterers begin here while the painters grid the antechamber."

Kasa nodded. "And the lamp house?"

"In the corridor," Menna said. "The heat will escape upward. The reflectors will push light into the burial chamber."

The scribe wrote quickly.

They inspected the treasury and annex, noting the cramped spaces, the low ceilings, the awkward angles. Every detail mattered. Every measurement would shape the work to come.

By the time they emerged from the tomb, the sun was high and the bowl of rock was bright with heat.

By dusk, the encampment had begun to take shape. Two tents stood on the flattest ledge. Water jars lined the shaded wall. The latrine trench was dug and lined with stones. The guards had marked the perimeter.

The leaders gathered around a small fire, the scribe sitting cross legged with his tablet.

Menna stood over them, hands clasped behind his back.

"Report."

Hapu spoke first. "The antechamber will take twelve plasterers at once. No more. The room is too narrow."

Kasa added, "The burial chamber can take eight painters on scaffolding, four on the floor."

Another leader said, "The corridor will need steps cut into the debris. And a rope line for safety."

The scribe recorded:

plaster volume estimates
lamp oil consumption
wick bundles needed per day
scaffold lengths
number of cedar poles
number of acacia poles
rope lengths
water jar counts
team rotation schedules
night shift requirements

Menna listened, nodding occasionally, correcting a number here, adjusting a sequence there.

When the fire burned low, he dismissed them.

"Sleep. Tomorrow the mountain wakes."

Nebre waited for him at the edge of the encampment, a small bundle of linen under his arm.

"Grandfather," he said softly. "I brought your cloak."

Menna took it, draping it over his shoulders. The night air was cooling quickly.

Nebre hesitated. "Is it... is it dangerous? Inside?"

Menna looked toward the dark mouth of the tomb, now silent again.

"It is always dangerous," he said. "But danger is not the enemy. Carelessness is."

Nebre nodded, absorbing the lesson.

Menna placed a hand on the boy's shoulder. "Tomorrow you will see the full workforce arrive. One hundred thirty men and women. They will look to us for order. For safety. For purpose."

Nebre swallowed. "And I will help?"

Menna smiled faintly. "You already have."

They stood together in the quiet, the valley stretching out before them, the cliffs glowing faintly under the rising stars.

Behind them, the unfinished tomb waited — no longer sleeping, but listening.

Chapter 6: The Tomb Stirs

The village woke before the sun.

The sound was familiar—the low murmur of voices, the steady grind of tools against stone, the shuffle of sandals along packed earth—but something within it had changed. The rhythm held tighter now. Less idle. Less forgiving.

What had once been motion had become purpose.

Word had spread, yes—but it no longer moved. It had settled.

The king was dead.

And the mountain waited.

Menna stepped into the courtyard as the first pale light touched the eastern ridge. He paused, not to observe—as he had done before—but to measure the silence between sounds. It told him more than the voices themselves.

Yesterday, the workers had gathered from habit, from duty.

Today, they came with knowledge.

The difference was subtle, but it pressed on everything.

The eight teams formed as they always had, but closer now. Their lines tighter. Their speech more restrained. Where before there had been small exchanges—nods, gestures, the quiet ease of men accustomed to their work—there was now a kind of restraint, as if each word carried weight that did not belong to the speaker alone.

Nebre stood near the forecourt, watching them in the same way he always had, though even he seemed to see something new in their arrangement. He did not move to call them to order. He did not need to.

They were already ready.

Menna moved among them without speaking. He passed the tool bearers, the water carriers, the cutters, each man acknowledging him with a small shift of posture rather than voice. It was enough.

No one asked what would come next.

They understood.

The path to the valley lay as it always had, cut into the stone by centuries of passage. Yet as they began to move, it no longer felt like a road taken, but one entered.

The ascent was steady.

Where once there had been the small interruptions of work—the halting of movement, the repositioning of burden, the exchange of brief words—there was now continuity. No pause long enough to break the rhythm. Even the donkeys, laden and patient, stepped with an odd certainty, as though the line itself carried them forward.

The valley opened before them slowly, not revealing itself all at once, but in layers of pale stone and shadow. The air held its usual stillness, but it seemed less empty now, as though something unseen had begun to occupy the space.

The tomb stood where it had stood for generations before them.

Unfinished.

Waiting.

Menna halted just short of the entrance, as he had done the day before. But where he had once considered the structure before him—the alignment, the cut, the integrity of the work—his attention now turned elsewhere.

Time had entered the space.

It moved differently here, not marked by the passing of light alone, but by the narrowing of it.

They would not work at their pace.

They would work at its.

Behind him, the teams arranged themselves without instruction. It was not haste that guided them, but precision born from the understanding that there would be no second attempt at what they had begun.

Stone would not forgive error.

Nor would memory.

Nebre approached, stopping at Menna's side. He did not speak immediately. His gaze followed the line of the entrance, down into the shadow where the work would continue.

"They feel it," he said at last, his voice low.

Menna did not turn.

"Yes."

Neither man needed to say more.

The tools were set.

The first strikes began—not as the scattered sounds of beginning labor, but as a continuation of something already in motion. Each impact echoed deeper than before, carried further along the cut walls of the passage.

The tomb had begun to answer.

Menna stepped forward into the threshold.

The light behind him narrowed, the air cooling as the stone enclosed around him. He did not pause at the entrance this time.

There was no need to look back.

The work ahead would shape itself from what they carried into it—not only the tools, nor the strength of their hands, but the understanding that what they built would remain long after the voices that filled the valley had faded.

He placed his hand briefly against the stone.

Not to test it.

But to feel its silence.

Then he gave the first order of the day.

And the mountain received it.

Chapter 7: The Ascent

The path from Set Maat to the Valley was short in distance but long in effort.

It began gently enough – a narrow lane between mudbrick walls, shaded by reed awnings and cluttered with morning life. Women called after their children, reminding them to stay close. Toddlers clung to their mothers' skirts, wide eyed at the sight of so many tools and donkeys. Older children ran ahead, eager to be useful, carrying small bundles of cord or empty jars.

But once the village fell behind, the land rose sharply.

The path became a twisting ribbon of pale limestone, broken in places, sloping in others, always climbing. The sun had barely cleared the eastern ridge, yet the heat already pressed against the backs of the workers.

Donkeys brayed and stamped, their hooves scraping against the rock. They were sure footed, but even they struggled on the steeper turns. One slipped on a patch of loose gravel, stumbling sideways into another. The second donkey lurched, its load of gypsum sacks shifting dangerously.

"Hold him!" a handler shouted.

Two men rushed forward, grabbing the packsaddle and steadying the animal before it toppled. The gypsum sacks settled with a soft thud.

Menna turned at the commotion. "Check the lashings."

The handler nodded, tightening the ropes. "The slope is worse than last season."

"It will be worse still near the bowl," Menna said. "Keep them spaced."

The caravan moved on.

Women walked in clusters, balancing water jars on their hips or carrying baskets of bread and dried fish. Some had infants tied to their backs with linen slings. Others held the hands of small children who insisted on walking, their little legs pumping furiously to keep up.

Nebre walked beside Menna, chalk and cord tucked under his arm. He watched the donkeys with fascination — the way they leaned into the slope, the way their ears flicked at every sound.

"Grandfather," he said, "why do they not use horses? They are faster."

Menna smiled faintly. "Horses are fast on flat ground. But here?" He gestured to the narrow path, the loose stones, the steep drop to one side. "A horse would panic. A donkey knows the mountain."

Nebre nodded, absorbing the lesson.

Ahead of them, the clearing team had already reached the first ridge. The rope man paused to look back, gauging the distance between his group and the main caravan. The scribe stood beside him, tablet in hand, recording the time.

Behind Menna, the eight team leaders kept their units in tight formation.

The plasterers carried their tools wrapped in linen. The painters protected their brushes in reed cases. The draughtsmen held their chalk boards close. The lamp tenders guarded the alabaster boxes like newborns. The scaffold builders carried cedar poles on their shoulders. The tool sharpeners walked with bundles of whetstones. The water carriers balanced jars with practiced ease. The donkey handlers moved constantly, adjusting loads, calming animals, calling warnings.

It was not chaos. It was a living machine.

But even a machine could falter.

At a narrow bend, a donkey balked, refusing to move. Its ears flattened, its hooves scraping backward. The handler tugged gently, murmuring encouragement, but the animal braced itself stubbornly.

"Give him space," Menna called.

The line behind the donkey shifted, men stepping aside, women pulling children close. The animal snorted, stamped, then finally moved forward, reassured by the open path.

Nebre exhaled. "Even the donkeys know this is important."

Menna placed a hand on the boy's shoulder. "They know the weight they carry."

The path steepened again.

The valley walls rose around them, blocking the view ahead. The tomb could not be seen from below — only the bowl of rock at the top of the slope, hidden until the final turn. The workers climbed in silence now, the only sounds the scrape of sandals, the clink of jars, the soft grunt of donkeys.

At last, the clearing team came into view, small figures against the pale stone. They had reached the bowl and were already cutting the first steps into the debris slope. The rope man anchored himself against the wall, feeding out the line slowly. The lamp carrier held the alabaster box high, its soft glow barely visible in the morning light.

Menna stopped at the ridge, letting the caravan gather behind him.

"This is where the work begins," he said.

The workers looked up at the bowl — the steep slope, the half buried entrance, the narrow ledge where tents would stand, the rough ground where water jars would be placed.

Some swallowed hard. Some whispered prayers. Some simply stared, measuring the task ahead.

Nebre stepped closer to Menna. "It looks smaller than I imagined."

Menna nodded. "It always does. Until you stand inside."

Panehsy raised his staff.

"Teams to your positions!"

The forecourt of the tomb site erupted into motion — but now with purpose sharpened by proximity. Donkeys were led to the flattest ground. Women set down their jars. Men unwrapped tools. The eight leaders spread out, directing their units with clipped commands.

Menna watched it all, the mountain wind tugging at his cloak.

Behind him, the village was already out of sight. Ahead of him, the tomb waited – silent, unfinished, and demanding.

The ascent was over. The real work was about to begin.

Chapter 8: Clearing the Slope

The clearing team reached the bowl first.

By the time the main caravan arrived, the four men were already halfway up the debris slope, cutting the first steps into the unstable mixture of sand, gravel, and stone. The rope man had anchored himself against the wall, feeding out the line slowly, testing each foothold before shifting his weight. The lamp carrier held the alabaster box high, its glow faint in the morning light but steady enough to guide the cutters.

Menna watched from the ridge as the main workforce gathered behind him. The bowl looked deceptively small from above — a shallow depression carved by centuries of rare but violent rain. But the slope was treacherous, and the debris inside the corridor was worse.

"Teams to your positions!" Panehsy called.

The workers spread out across the ledge, unloading donkeys, stacking tools, and marking the ground where tents and water jars would stand. The eight leaders moved among them, directing with clipped commands.

Menna stepped forward.

"Bring the rope coils," he said. "And the cedar poles."

Nebre hurried to fetch them, his arms full of chalk, cord, and a small wooden board. He nearly tripped on a loose stone but caught himself, cheeks flushing. Menna pretended not to notice.

The clearing team paused as Menna approached the slope.

"How is it?" he asked.

The lead cutter wiped sweat from his brow. "Loose. Too loose. Every step collapses unless we brace it."

"Then brace it," Menna said. "Use the cedar halves. Drive them into the slope."

The cutter nodded and signaled to the rope man, who fed out more line. The men hammered the cedar stakes into the debris, creating small ledges that held long enough for the next step to be cut.

Nebre stood beside Menna, watching intently.

"Grandfather," he whispered, "why not clear from the top? Why not pull the debris out with baskets?"

Menna shook his head. "Because the slope will collapse. The debris must be cut from within, not dragged from above. The mountain must be persuaded, not forced."

Nebre nodded, absorbing the lesson.

A shout rose from the slope.

One of the cutters had slipped – his foot sinking into a pocket of loose gravel. The rope jerked taut as the rope man braced himself, digging his heels into the wall. The cutter dangled for a moment, arms flailing, before finding purchase again.

Menna's voice cut through the air. "Slow your pace. Test every step. The mountain is patient – you must be more so."

The cutter nodded, breathless.

Behind them, the main workforce continued to unload supplies. A donkey stumbled as its load shifted, nearly knocking over a stack of water jars. A handler grabbed the animal's bridle, murmuring softly until it calmed.

Children clung to their mothers' skirts, wide eyed at the sight of the slope and the men climbing it. One little girl pointed at the alabaster light box.

"Why is the light so soft?" she asked.

"For inside," she said.

Menna heard her and felt a quiet satisfaction. Even the smallest child understood the purpose of the light.

The clearing team reached the breach at Door One. The rope man secured the line to a cedar stake driven deep into the slope. The lamp carrier held the light box close to the opening, illuminating the narrow corridor beyond.

Menna climbed the slope carefully, Nebre following close behind.

Inside the breach, the air was cool and still. The debris rose almost to Menna's chest, sloping downward toward Door Two. The ceiling pressed low, the limestone layers pale and unbroken.

"Mark the slope," Menna said.

Nebre knelt, chalk in hand, and drew a line along the wall at shoulder height.

"Again," Menna said. "Every two cubits."

Nebre moved forward, marking the wall at regular intervals. His hand trembled slightly, but the lines were straight.

The cutters began clearing the first section of the corridor, scooping debris into baskets and passing them back along the slope. The baskets were carried out by the water carriers, who dumped the debris onto the ledge outside.

The air filled with dust.

The lamp carrier adjusted the copper disk, angling the light deeper into the corridor. The narrow beam illuminated the rough walls, the uneven floor, the half buried doorway ahead.

Menna studied the light carefully.

"The lamp house must be built here," he said, pointing to a small alcove near the breach. "The heat will rise. The smoke will escape through the upper cracks. The reflectors will push the light forward."

Hapu nodded. "We will need more copper disks."

"And more wicks," Menna said. "And more oil. The corridor will drink it."

The scribe recorded everything.

A sudden rumble echoed through the corridor.

The cutters froze.

A small cascade of gravel slid down the slope, bouncing off the cedar stakes. The rope man tightened his grip, eyes wide.

Menna raised a hand. "Hold."

The rumble faded. The ceiling remained still.

"Continue," Menna said softly. "But with care."

The men resumed their work, slower now, more deliberate.

Nebre looked up at Menna. "Will it collapse?"

"Not today," Menna said. "Not if we respect it."

Outside, the sun climbed higher. The workers moved in steady rhythm, carrying debris, adjusting loads, tending donkeys, mixing plaster, sharpening tools.

Inside, the clearing team carved the first safe path into the tomb.

By midday, the first ten cubits of the corridor were cleared. The slope was stable. The rope line was secure. The lamp house location was chosen.

Menna stepped back into the sunlight, dust clinging to his skin.

Panehsy approached. "Progress?"

"Good," Menna said. "Slow, but good. The mountain is cooperating."

Panehsy nodded. "And the boy?"

Menna glanced at Nebre, who was wiping chalk dust from his hands.

"He learns," Menna said. "And he listens."

Panehsy smiled faintly. "Then he will serve the king well."

Menna looked toward the bowl, where the workers continued their steady labor.

"The king will have his house," he said quietly.

And the mountain, for the first time in years, began to open.

Chapter 9: The Second Morning

Dawn came cold.

The sun had not yet cleared the eastern ridge when the first sounds of the camp stirred the bowl awake — the soft braying of donkeys, the clink of tack, the low murmur of men rising from their blankets. Smoke drifted from the small hearths where women coaxed last night's embers back to life, feeding them with handfuls of dry brush. The air smelled of ash, donkey dung, sweat, and the faint mineral tang of gypsum dust.

A dog trotted between the tents, nose low, searching for scraps. A second dog barked once, sharp and impatient, before settling beside the donkey line. A cat — thin, dust colored, half feral — leapt onto a crate and watched the camp with slow, blinking eyes.

Men stretched stiffly, rubbing sleep from their faces. A few walked to the latrine trench at the far edge of the bowl, where the ground sloped away. They used smooth stones or handfuls of sand, muttering at the cold. Others washed their hands and faces with water poured from jars, the shock of it waking them fully.

Children woke next — whining, laughing, stumbling sleepily toward their mothers. A little boy cried until a woman pressed a warm piece of bread into his hand. A girl carried a small jar of water to her father, proud of her task. The camp filled with the soft chaos of morning life.

The donkeys grew restless as the light strengthened. They stamped, shook their heads, and brayed, tugging at their ropes. Handlers moved among them, checking hooves, tightening straps, murmuring reassurance. One donkey kicked at another, and the two animals bumped hard, sending a stack of empty baskets tumbling. A handler cursed softly and separated them.

The sun crested the ridge.

Warmth spilled into the bowl.

The day began.

The air inside the corridor was cool and stale, carrying the faint scent of dust and old stone. No deadly gases — only the breath of a place long sealed. Dust motes drifted in the lamplight as the lamp tenders trimmed wicks and tested the copper reflectors.

The first corridor was clear now — the debris slope cut into steps, the rope line secured, the walls marked with chalk. The floor was uneven but passable. The ceiling pressed low, forcing taller men to stoop.

The lamplight stretched down the cleared corridor in a thin, steady beam, catching dust that drifted like drifting ash. Nebre followed close behind Menna, chalk and cord in hand, trying not to step on his grandfather's heels.

"Begin here," Menna said, placing his palm against the wall just inside Door One.

Nebre knelt, waiting.

Menna tapped the floor with his foot, then lifted his hand to the ceiling. "Measure it the way your body understands," he said. "A man's height. A hand's width. A finger's breadth. These are the oldest measures in Kemet."

Nebre nodded, relieved. The numbers made sense now – not foreign, not strange, just the language of the body.

Menna stretched the cord from floor to ceiling. "Six full hand spans and part of another," he said. "Mark it."

Nebre drew a clean line. The chalk squeaked softly.

They moved deeper into the corridor. The walls pressed closer; the ceiling dipped. Menna ducked beneath the low point and tapped the stone with his knuckles.

"Here," he said. "Five and a half hand spans above your head. Too low for a full frame. We'll need short poles – acacia, not cedar."

Nebre wrote the note on his board. "Why not cedar?"

"Cedar is for long spans," Menna said. "Straight, strong, and precious. Acacia bends. It fits where the mountain refuses to give."

They reached the turn. The corridor bent sharply toward Door Two, the lamplight catching the roughness of the wall.

"This turn is the trouble," Menna murmured. "The scaffolding must bend with it."

Nebre stretched the cord across the angle. "Seven long steps from the corner to the door."

"Seven," Menna repeated. "Enough for two men to work, but not enough for mistakes."

Nebre hesitated. "Grandfather... have you built scaffolding in a king's tomb before?"

Menna paused, his hand resting on the wall. The lamplight softened his expression.

"No," he said quietly. "Not for a king. But I have seen the drafts. The sketches. The plans kept in the foremen's house. I have studied the marks left by those who came before us – the lines they drew, the heights they measured, the places where their scaffolding stood."

He traced a faint groove in the stone with his fingertip.

"Every tomb teaches the next," he said. "Even when the men who built it are long gone."

Nebre swallowed. "And this one?"

"This one," Menna said, "will teach you."

He stepped back, surveying the corridor with a craftsman's eye.

"We will build a narrow scaffold here," he said. "Just a plank on two short poles. Enough to reach the ceiling. Enough to mark the grid. Enough to see how the mountain breathes."

Nebre frowned slightly, looking at the rough limestone above them. "Grandfather... why plaster here at all? No one will see this corridor."

Menna smiled, the kind of smile that held both patience and memory. "Plaster is not for beauty alone," he said. "It is for truth."

He tapped the wall with his knuckles. The sound was uneven, hollow in places, solid in others.

"The stone here is rough," Menna continued. "Uneven. It shifts. If we paint directly on it, the lines wander. The gods deserve straight lines, even in places where no eyes will ever look."

Nebre nodded slowly.

"And plaster tells us where the mountain is weak," Menna added. "A crack in plaster is a warning. A crack in stone is a danger. We learn the difference by laying the first coat."

Nebre looked up again, seeing the wall differently now – not as a surface, but as a message.

Menna stepped back, his gaze drifting not to the corridor but somewhere far beyond it. "In the foremen's house," he said softly, "there were sketches of older tombs. Not full drawings – just marks, notes, reminders. A line showing where the ceiling dipped. A symbol for a weak seam. A measure for how high the scaffold must stand."

He traced a faint groove in the stone with his fingertip.

"I remember one sketch from the tomb of Thutmose's steward," he said. "A narrow corridor like this one. The plasterers wrote: 'Too tight for full frame. Use short poles. Mark ceiling first.'"

Nebre's eyes widened. "They left notes?"

"Not for us," Menna said. "For themselves. For the next team. For the craft. Knowledge is passed in marks and memory."

He gestured to the ceiling. "And now it is our turn."

Nebre swallowed, feeling the weight of it.

Menna continued, "We plaster this corridor because the king's house must be whole. Even the unseen parts. Even the narrow places. The plaster binds the stone. The grid guides the painters. The scaffold lets us reach what the mountain hides."

He placed a hand on Nebre's shoulder.

"And you will learn it all. Not because you are my grandson – but because the work demands it."

Nebre nodded, gripping the chalk with new purpose.

Menna turned back to the wall. "Come. The mountain waits for no one."

The lamp tenders placed the alabaster light box in the alcove Menna had chosen the day before. They adjusted the copper disk, angling it to push the light deeper into the corridor. The glow was soft but steady, illuminating the plaster blocking of Door Two.

Hapu and Kasa stood before the sealed doorway, studying the plaster.

"The stamps are intact," Hapu said. "No cracks. No pry marks."

Kasa tapped the surface lightly. "Solid. Two coats again. They sealed this one with more care."

Nebre leaned closer. "Will we preserve the seals?"

"Some," Menna said. "Not all. We need a clean breach."

The scribe recorded everything.

Menna walked the length of the corridor again, counting steps, measuring angles, marking where scaffolding would need to stand. He paused at the turn leading toward the antechamber.

"The ceiling slopes here," he said. "We will need angled braces."

Hapu nodded. "Acacia for the braces. Cedar for the main poles."

"And planks?" Menna asked.

"Enough for now," Kasa said. "But not enough for the full chamber."

Menna ran his hand along the wall, feeling the roughness beneath the chalk lines. "We will need more cedar before the week is out."

Nebre looked up. "From the warehouse?"

"Yes," Menna said. "The long poles. The straight ones. The ones from Lebanon."

"How long is the journey?"

"Half a day by donkey," Menna said. "If the handlers hurry."

Nebre nodded, committing the distance to memory.

The lamp tenders lit the first test flame. The alabaster box glowed softly, the copper disk catching the light and sending it forward in a narrow beam. Shadows danced along the walls.

The workers fell silent.

For the first time, the tomb breathed light.

Menna stood at the center of the corridor, hands clasped behind his back, eyes narrowed in thought. The light flickered across his face, catching the lines of concentration.

He saw everything:

the slope of the ceiling
the unevenness of the floor
the distance between Door One and Door Two
the angle of the turn
the height of the walls

the places where scaffolding must stand
the places where it must bend
the places where it must not touch

He calculated wood lengths in his head.

"Three long cedar poles," he murmured. "Four medium. Six short. Eight planks. Two angled braces. And rope. Twice what we have."

He turned to Hapu. "Send two donkeys back to the warehouse. They must return before sunset."

Hapu nodded and left.

Menna looked at Nebre. "You will help measure the antechamber when we breach Door Two."

Nebre's eyes widened. "Me?"

"You," Menna said. "You must learn the mountain. It will not wait for you."

Nebre swallowed and nodded.

Menna placed a hand on the boy's shoulder. "Come. The day is short."

Outside, the camp bustled with life. Inside, the tomb waited in silence. And Menna stood between them — the mind that would shape the king's house.

CHAPTER 10: BREACH OF DOOR TWO

The morning sun had climbed high enough to spill light into the upper steps of the bowl, but the corridor beyond Door One remained cool and dim. The lamp house glowed softly in its alcove, the copper reflector pressing a narrow beam forward toward the sealed doorway at the far end.

Menna stood before Door Two with Hapu, Kasa, and Nebre at his side.

The gypsum blocking was smooth and pale, stamped again and again with the jackal over the nine bound captives. The impressions were crisp, untouched. No hand had disturbed them since the day the original builders sealed this abandoned tomb—decades before Tutankhamun was even born.

Nebre felt the weight of it: the stillness, the expectation, the breath of a place that had been waiting.

Menna ran his fingertips along the gypsum surface.

"Two coats," he murmured. "A rough bedding beneath, a fine sealing layer above. They closed this one with care."

Kasa nodded. "More care than the first."

"Because this door leads inward," Menna said quietly. "Into a chamber no one has seen in a lifetime."

The workers behind them fell silent.

Menna stepped back, studying the face of the gypsum seal.

"We cut a small breach first," he said. "High, near the corner. Enough for a lamp. Enough for an eye."

He rested his palm against the sealed face of the second door. It felt cool—almost calm—despite the work and breathing around them.

Nebre watched his hand, then the stamps pressed into the surface: the jackal, the bound figures, softened by time but still present.

"Grandfather," he said softly, "how does it still hold?"

Menna did not answer at once. He leaned in, close enough that his breath brushed the gypsum.

"Because it was never meant to be hurried," he said at last. "They mixed the gypsum mortar thick. Pressed it deep. They sealed it knowing water might come, knowing stone shifts, knowing the mountain remembers force."

He tapped the gypsum mortar lightly with his knuckles—not to test it, but to listen.

"Material like this doesn't fail all at once," he continued. "It gives where it must, then tightens again. The water runs past it. The weight leans on it. And still it waits."

Nebre frowned. "So it's strong?"

Menna smiled, just slightly. "It is patient."

"Here," Menna said, setting the chisel into the upper corner. "Above the weight."

He straightened, took the chisel from Hapu's hand, and set its edge carefully into the upper corner.

“That is why we do not tear it open,” he said. “We ask. And we wait for the place it is willing to let go.”

The chisel remained poised. The door said nothing.

Then Menna nodded.

“Now.”

Nebre swallowed. “Will I see it?”

Menna looked at him. “You will hold the lamp.”

Nebre’s breath caught.

Hapu unwrapped the fine chisels—slender, sharp, their handles carved with family emblems. Kasa selected one, turning it once, then tested its edge with his thumb.

“Begin here,” Menna said, indicating the upper corner. “Preserve the lower seals. Panehsy will want them intact.”

Kasa set the chisel against the gypsum seal. Nebre held the lamp steady, the flame trembling slightly in the still air.

“Strike,” Menna said.

The mallet fell with a soft, precise tap.

A thin crack appeared.

Another tap. Another.

The gypsum mortar began to flake, delicate as eggshell. Pale dust drifted down in slow curls.

Nebre brought the lamp closer, angling the light into the widening breach. The flame flickered, shadows shifting across the stamped surface.

Kasa worked slowly, carefully, widening the opening no larger than a man’s fist. The gypsum fell away in controlled fragments, each piece caught before it touched the floor.

The air behind the door stirred faintly—a breath of coolness, dry and ancient, untouched since the day the original workers walked away and left this place to the mountain.

Menna leaned close. "Stop."

Kasa stepped back.

Menna peered through the opening. Nebre lifted the lamp higher, pressing the light into the darkness beyond.

At first, there was nothing—only shadow.

Then the light found its edge.

A wall. Smooth. Gypsum-coated. Unfinished. Waiting.

Nebre gasped softly.

Menna's voice dropped to a whisper. "The antechamber."

Behind them, the workers shifted, murmuring prayers under their breath—not fear, but recognition.

Menna straightened. "We widen the breach. Slowly. No collapse. No rush."

Hapu and Kasa resumed, alternating strikes, widening the opening handspan by handspan. The gypsum fell in clean sections, each piece passed back in baskets to keep the floor clear.

When the breach was wide enough for a man to pass, Menna raised his hand.

"No one enters yet."

He turned to Nebre. "Bring the measuring board."

Nebre hurried to fetch it, his hands trembling with excitement.

Menna knelt at the threshold, studying the exposed edges.

"The stone behind the seal is sound," he said. "No cracks. No movement. The builders left this chamber unfinished—but stable."

Kasa nodded. "We can pass safely."

Menna turned to Nebre. "You will go first."

Nebre froze. "Me?"

"You are small," Menna said. "And careful. And the mountain must meet you before it meets the others."

Nebre swallowed hard, then nodded.

"Hold it steady," he said. "Do not touch the walls. Do not step beyond the first span until I say."

He turned to Kasa. "Bring the fiber rope."

Kasa moved quickly, returning with a coil of dark palm fiber line—worn smooth from years of handling. Menna took it, testing the weight with his hands, then looped it beneath Nebre's arms, crossing it once behind his back.

"Not tight," Menna said, adjusting the knot. "Just enough to catch you if the floor gives way."

Nebre nodded, breath shallow but steady.

Menna glanced back toward Hapu and the two men braced behind him. "If I pull twice," he said, "you lift. No questions."

The rope went taut in their hands.

Menna's palm rested briefly on Nebre's shoulder. "Now."

Nebre stepped forward.

The workers held their breath.

Menna guided him to the opening, lowering from the shoulders, feeling the line take Nebre's weight a little at a time. Nebre ducked, lifted the lamp, and slid through the breach as if easing into water.

Light spilled into the antechamber.

The rope remained firm. The men above waited.

Nebre stopped.

His breath caught.

The room was larger than he expected—cold, silent, untouched. Dust lay thick across the floor, unbroken for decades. The air felt older than anything he had ever breathed.

"Grandfather..." he whispered. "It's empty."

Menna's voice remained calm. "Describe it."

Nebre swallowed. "Rough walls. Unfinished gypsum coating. Builder's marks. The floor dips in the far corner. And... it feels like no one has been here since the day they left."

Menna closed his eyes for a moment.

This was no longer the abandoned tomb of a forgotten official.

This was now the space that must become the king's eternal house.

He opened his eyes.

"We begin."

Chapter 11: The First Hours

The rope went slack.

Menna exhaled, letting the tension leave his shoulders as Nebre's voice drifted back through the breach.

"It's empty," the boy had said. Empty — but waiting.

Menna rose slowly, dusting gypsum from his hands. "We withdraw," he said. "All of us. Back to the first door."

The men obeyed at once. They filed out of the corridor in single line, shoulders brushing the narrow walls, tools held close to avoid scraping the fresh chalk marks. The lamp house remained lit behind them, its glow stretching thinly down the cleared passage like a thread of captured sunlight.

At the top of the steps, the waiting workers straightened. Some had been there since dawn, watching the bowl for any sign, listening for the faintest echo from below.

Hapu emerged first, then Kasa, then Nebre — still holding the lamp, still breathing the cold air of the chamber he had just seen. Menna came last, sealing the moment with his presence.

A murmur rippled through the gathered men.

"Is it safe?" "What lies beyond?" "Is the chamber sound?"

Menna lifted the gypsum seal fragment he carried — a clean, stamped piece from the upper corner of

Door Two. The jackal and the nine bound captives were still visible, though softened by time.

"This," he said, "goes to the chief builder. He will take it to Panehsy. The temple will know the tomb is open and ready to be prepared."

A runner stepped forward, bowed, and received the fragment with both hands before sprinting up the slope toward the Valley path.

Menna turned back to the men.

"We have work."

The words settled over them like a command and a blessing.

They descended again — not into mystery this time, but into labor.

The corridor between Door One and Door Two was still half filled with the debris slope they had carved into steps. Now it had to be cleared entirely.

Menna stood at the top of the slope, marking positions with the end of his staff.

"Here. And here. And here. One man every three paces. No crowding. No slipping."

The men took their places, forming a narrow human chain from the breach at Door Two all the way to the sunlight above.

"Baskets only half full," Menna said. "We do not spill. We do not rush. The mountain punishes haste."

Kasa and Hapu stationed themselves at the breach, breaking down the remaining gypsum fragments and loading them into baskets. Nebre placed three small lamps on the floor — one at the breach, one at the midpoint, one near Door One —

their flames steady and low, marking the safe path for feet and hands.

The first basket passed from hand to hand, moving upward in a slow, steady rhythm. Then another. Then another.

The corridor filled with the soft scrape of sandals, the muted thud of baskets, the quiet breath of men working in close quarters.

Menna watched the line, adjusting positions, correcting grips, shifting men where the slope dipped too sharply.

"This is the spine of the work," he said to Nebre. "If the line fails, the tomb fails."

Nebre nodded, eyes wide, absorbing everything.

When the first hour of clearing was underway, Menna returned to the breach. He ducked inside, Nebre close behind him, the rope still tied loosely around the boy's chest.

The antechamber greeted them with the same cold stillness as before. Dust lay thick across the floor, unbroken except for Nebre's careful footprints.

Menna checked the wick through the narrow slit in the alabaster. "Trimmed clean," he said. "Enough oil for the first look. No more."

The light spread outward, revealing more of the unfinished walls – rough gypsum, builder's marks, faint grid lines abandoned mid stroke.

Nebre whispered, "It feels... older in here."

"It is," Menna said. "Older than the king. Older than us. Older than the men who cut it."

He knelt, pressing his palm to the floor. The dust was cold, almost damp with age.

"We measure," he said.

Nebre unrolled the cord. Menna took one end, walking to the far wall. The chamber swallowed the sound of his steps.

"Length," Menna said.

Nebre stretched the cord taut. "Twenty three long steps."

"Width."

"Thirteen."

"Ceiling height?"

Nebre looked up. "Just over a man's reach. A little more near the center."

Menna nodded. "Enough for scaffolding. Enough for the painters. Enough for the king."

He moved to the far corner where the floor dipped. "We will need fill here. Packed tight. No settling."

Nebre wrote the notes on his board, chalk whispering across the surface.

Menna stood in the center of the room, turning slowly, seeing not what was there but what must be.

"This chamber will hold the first offerings," he said. "The chests. The linens. The jars. The things he will need in the next world."

Nebre swallowed. "And we prepare it?"

"We prepare everything," Menna said. "Every wall. Every corner. Every breath of this place."

When they emerged again into the corridor, the conveyor line was moving smoothly. The debris pile at the top of the slope had grown into a mound. The sun had shifted, casting long shadows across the bowl.

A runner returned, breathless.

"Panehsy has received the seal," he said. "He sends word: the temple acknowledges the opening. The work is now under the protection of the gods."

Menna bowed his head once.

"Then we continue."

He turned to the men.

"By sunset, the corridor will be clear. By tomorrow, the chamber will be ready for plaster. And by the end of the week, the king's house will begin to take shape."

The men straightened, renewed.

Nebre looked at his grandfather, seeing not just a craftsman but the man who would guide the king's eternal home into being.

Menna lifted the lamp.

"Back to work."

Chapter 12: The Night Council

By the time the sun dipped behind the western ridge, the bowl was alive with firelight.

Small hearths flickered in a wide circle, each one claimed by a different team. The smell of lentils, onions, and smoke drifted through the cooling air. Donkeys settled in their lines. Children slept against their mothers. Dogs curled near the warmth of the stones.

Menna sat at the central fire, the largest of them all, where the team leaders gathered at the end of every day. Nebre sat beside him, chalk board in his lap, listening.

The men arrived in twos and threes — plasterers, line drawers, pigment grinders, carpenters, lamp tenders, rope men, water carriers. Each team carried its own rhythm, its own jokes, its own lineage. Some families had worked together for generations; others had taken apprentices from neighbors or cousins.

Tonight, for the first time, they sat as one.

Hapu spoke first. "The corridor is clear. The breach is stable. The antechamber is sound."

A murmur of approval passed around the circle.

Menna nodded. "Tomorrow we begin the rotation."

The men straightened. This was the moment they had been waiting for — and dreading.

Menna lifted a stick and drew a circle in the dust.

"This is the tomb," he said. "And this—" he drew a line through the circle "—is the time we do not have."

The men leaned closer.

"We work in teams," Menna said. "Eight teams. Each one complete. Each one capable of every task."

He pointed to the first group — the plasterers.

"You will lay the rough coat."

He pointed to the next — the line drawers.

"You will mark the grid."

Then the painters.

"You will lay the first colors."

Then the finishers.

"You will seal the work."

He looked around the circle.

"But you will not do these things in order. You will do them in rotation."

The men nodded. They knew this rhythm — it was the same used in the great tombs of the nobles, but never with such urgency.

Menna continued.

"Each team will work for one hour. No more. No less. When your hour ends, you step aside. The next team enters. They take your place. They continue your work as if they were your own hands."

Nebre watched the men's faces — the pride, the fear, the understanding.

Menna drew eight marks around the circle.

"These are your hours. Day and night. Without pause. Without delay. The king's house must be ready before the embalmers finish their work."

A silence settled over the fire.

Everyone knew what that meant.

Seventy days. No more. No forgiveness.

Menna lifted his head.

"You will sleep in shifts. You will eat in shifts. You will return to the village only when your body demands it. Your families will understand. They have done this before."

A few men nodded — the older ones, the ones who remembered the tombs of earlier kings.

Menna continued.

"Each team is a family. Some by blood. Some by craft. Some by choice. But once you enter the tomb, you are one body. One breath. One purpose."

He looked at Nebre.

"And the apprentices will learn from all of you."

Nebre felt the weight of that — the honor and the burden.

Hapu leaned forward. "How many men at a time?"

"Twelve," Menna said. "No more. The chamber is too small. The air too still. Twelve men can work. Thirteen will stumble."

Kasa added, "And the lamp tenders?"

"Two," Menna said. "Always two. One for the light box. One for the wicks."

A murmur of agreement.

Menna drew another line in the dust.

"The first team enters at sunrise. The second waits in the antechamber. The third waits at Door One. The fourth waits at the top of the steps. The others rest. When your hour comes, you move forward. When it ends, you move back."

He looked around the circle.

"This is the rhythm. This is the order. This is how we finish a king's house in time."

The fire crackled. Sparks rose into the darkening sky.

One of the younger painters spoke. "And if a team falters?"

Menna's voice was steady. "Then the next team carries them. And the next. And the next. Until the work is done."

Another silence — deeper this time, heavier.

Menna placed the stick aside.

"Tonight, you rest. Tomorrow, you become the mountain's heartbeat."

The men rose slowly, each returning to his own fire, his own family, his own thoughts. Some spoke quietly. Some sharpened tools. Some stared into the flames, imagining the hours ahead.

Nebre remained beside Menna.

"Grandfather," he said softly, "how do they know where to stand? When to move? When to stop?"

Menna smiled — tired, but proud.

"Because they have done this all their lives," he said. "And because tomorrow, they do it for a king."

Nebre looked toward the dark mouth of the tomb.

The mountain waited.

And now, so did they.

Chapter 13: The First Light

Dawn broke on the third day with two sounds rising from the bowl: the sharp rhythm of carpenters cutting wood, and the softer, deliberate movements of the stonewrights unwrapping alabaster.

Nebre stood beside Menna, watching the preparations unfold in the pale morning light. The air was cool, still holding the night's quiet, but the bowl was already alive with purpose.

Long, linen wrapped bundles lay on reed mats near the central fire. The stonewrights of Ptah knelt beside them, loosening the bindings with careful hands. One by one, the alabaster panels emerged — translucent, cool, and faintly glowing as the rising sun touched their surfaces.

Menna ran his fingertips along the edges.

"These are the lamp walls," he said. "Handle them with care."

The carpenters approached with the wooden cradle they had built in the night — a sturdy frame of cedar and acacia, its joints lashed tight with palmfiber rope. They set it down gently, and the stonewrights carried the alabaster panels through Door One and into the annex, where the space widened enough for careful work.

Nebre followed behind them, holding a small alabaster lamp to light their way.

Reed mats were laid on the floor. The wrappings were loosened. The alabaster panels were set out in a careful arc, their edges catching the lamplight.

The carpenters brought forward the wooden cradle. The stonewrights knelt, aligning the panels with practiced hands, sliding each one into its place with soft, muted clicks. The lamp took shape slowly, deliberately, like a sacred object remembering itself.

A jar of pale oil sat beside them, sealed with a clay stopper marked with the temple's sign.

"The Oil of First Light," Menna said quietly. "Only the lamp tenders touch it."

Two lamp tenders stepped forward, broke the seal, and poured a thin stream of the oil into the central basin. The wick was lowered, trimmed, and lit.

The alabaster walls glowed from within — warm, steady, impossibly even. The annex brightened as though the stone itself had awakened.

Four men lifted the assembled lamp, carrying it through the annex and toward the antechamber with slow, deliberate steps. Nebre followed behind them, his small lamp trembling in his hands.

The mountain seemed to hold its breath.

Inside the antechamber, the carpenters set down the scaffold pieces they had cut before dawn. Cedar for the long spans. Acacia for the short. Each piece measured against the marks Nebre had carried out the day before.

Menna directed them with quiet gestures.

"Here," he said. "Against the north wall. The ceiling dips there — use the short poles. Lash the crossbeam tight. No sway."

The carpenters worked quickly, assembling the scaffold with the ease of men who had done this all their lives. The frame rose in stages — poles set, planks laid, lashings tightened. When it stood firm, Menna tested it with his weight, pressing down with both hands.

"Good," he said. "It will hold."

The lamp tenders placed the chamber lamp on a low platform near the center of the room. Its glow spread outward, touching the unfinished walls with warm, steady light. The shadows softened. The room felt larger, clearer, almost awake.

Nebre exhaled slowly. "It's beautiful."

"It is necessary," Menna said. "Beauty comes later."

Before the first team stepped forward, the men paused at the threshold and reached for their headbands. Each one lifted the strip of leather from his belt — worn smooth from years of use — and tied it across his brow with practiced ease.

The copper disks were already mounted in their cradles, polished the night before until they caught even the faintest light. Nebre watched as the men adjusted the tilt of their disks, each one angling the reflector to catch the glow of the alabaster lamp. The diffused light struck the copper and scattered softly across the walls, turning the unfinished gypsum into a pale, living surface.

The team emblems — stamped feathers, lotus squares, family marks — gleamed faintly on the leather bands. No two were the same. Each one carried a lineage.

Menna nodded once. “Now you are ready.”

The first rotation team entered the antechamber in single file. Twelve men — no more. No less. Each one carrying the tools of his craft.

Menna raised his hand.

“This is the first hour,” he said. “The king’s house begins now.”

The plasterers stepped forward, mixing the first bowl of gypsum with water carried from the well. The smell of wet plaster filled the chamber — sharp, mineral, alive.

Menna watched the mixture carefully.

“Not too thin,” he said. “Not too dry. The wall must drink it.”

The plasterers pressed the first handfuls onto the north wall, smoothing it with wooden floats. The wet sheen caught the lamp’s glow, soft and steady.

Behind them, the scribes waited — chalk cords ready.

Behind the scribes, the painters waited — pigments ground fine.

Behind the painters, the finishers waited — brushes wrapped in linen.

The rotation had begun.

Menna stepped back, watching the room come alive.

The plasterers worked in steady strokes. The scribes snapped the first grid lines before the plaster fully set. The carpenters adjusted the scaffold as the work moved upward. The lamp tenders trimmed the wick. The painters prepared their bowls. The rope man checked the lashings. The water carrier refilled the jars.

Every man had a place. Every craft had a moment. Every moment depended on the one before it.

Nebre stood beside Menna, eyes wide.

“It’s like a heartbeat,” he whispered.

Menna nodded. “It is. And it must never stop.”

When the hour ended, Menna raised his hand.

“Step back.”

The first team withdrew, moving aside with practiced grace. The second team entered immediately, stepping into the footprints of the first, continuing the work as if they were the same hands.

The rotation was seamless.

The mountain had its rhythm now.

And Menna would keep it.

Chapter 14: The Ceiling Day

The chamber lamp was lit again before sunrise, its warm glow spreading across the fresh plaster of the burial chamber ceiling. The room felt different now – not empty, but expectant. Workers filed in quietly, their linen headbands tied, copper disks angled to catch the lamp's steady light.

Nebre stood beside Menna, holding a small alabaster lamp to guide the first team to their stations. The air smelled of gypsum dust and the faint sweetness of the Oil of First Light.

Reed mats were unrolled across the floor, overlapping slightly, forming a patchwork beneath the scaffold. Nebre had helped lay them out before dawn, smoothing the edges with his feet. They rustled softly as the men stepped across them.

Menna lifted his hand.

"Today we set the sky," he said.

The men nodded. They knew what that meant.

The scribes climbed the scaffold first, chalk cords looped over their shoulders. The planks creaked softly under their weight. Nebre watched them tilt their heads sideways, cheek nearly brushing the ceiling as they sighted the edge where wall met roof.

One scribe held the chalk coated red string in the corner. The other pulled it taut along the ceiling line.

Nebre whispered, "Why do they hold their heads like that?"

Menna answered without looking away. "To see the line true. The ceiling is never perfect. They must follow the wall, not the stone."

Nebre nodded, though he wasn't sure he understood.

"Hold," Menna said.

The chamber lamp glowed against the pale plaster, turning it a soft gold.

"Now."

The string snapped. A perfect red line appeared — sharp, clean, the first boundary of the king's eternal house.

The scribes shifted the scaffold, climbing down and up again, repeating the process around the room. Each snap echoed faintly, like a heartbeat.

When the last line was set, the painters stepped forward. They mixed the yellow pigment in shallow bowls, stirring it with wooden paddles until it thickened to the right consistency.

Nebre leaned close. "Why yellow?"

Menna smiled faintly. "Because it is the color of the sun. The color of gold. The color the king will wake to."

The first painter climbed the scaffold, dipped his brush, and swept the pigment across the ceiling. The stroke was broad, confident. Drops fell — tiny golden flecks landing on the reed mats below.

Nebre flinched. "It drips."

"Everything falls," Menna said. "Dust. Paint. Sweat. That is why the sky must be done first. If we painted the walls now, the ceiling would ruin them."

Nebre looked up again, watching the painter's arm move in long arcs. The yellow spread slowly, warming the room. The chamber lamp caught the fresh pigment, making it glow as though lit from within.

When the painters finished the first pass, Menna signaled to the apprentices. Three boys climbed the scaffold, each carrying a palm frond nearly as long as they were tall.

They began to fan the ceiling in slow, sweeping motions. Warm air rose from the lamp. The pigment dried in ripples of soft gold.

Nebre watched them, fascinated. "Does this help?"

Menna nodded. "It keeps the air moving. And it keeps dust from settling. A ceiling must dry clean."

The boys worked in silence, their fronds whispering against the warm air. The yellow deepened as it dried, turning richer, steadier.

Nebre hesitated before asking his next question.

"Will there be stars?"

Menna shook his head. "Not here."

"Why not?"

"In other tombs, yes. In the tomb of Userhat, the ceiling was blue with stars. They had years to work. And it was a nobleman's house, not a king's resting place."

He paused, watching the apprentices fan the ceiling.

"But here, the story is on the walls. The ceiling is the light that guides it. Plain, bright, and steady."

Nebre considered that. It made sense in a way he couldn't yet explain.

The rotation continued.

Painters climbed. Painters descended. New bowls of pigment were mixed. The lamp tenders trimmed the wick. The carpenters adjusted the scaffold height. The scribes checked the red boundary line again and again. The apprentices fanned the ceiling until their arms trembled.

The ceiling slowly transformed from pale plaster to warm gold.

Nebre carried water, fetched brushes, held lamps, and watched everything. He memorized the way Menna's eyes followed the painters' strokes, the way he tapped the scaffold to test its steadiness, the way he nodded when a line was true.

By late afternoon, the room glowed like dawn.

When the last painter climbed down, Menna stood in the center of the room and looked up. The chamber lamp illuminated the ceiling evenly, its glow reflecting off the copper disks of the workers' headbands.

Nebre stood beside him, exhausted but proud.

"It looks like the sun," he whispered.

Menna nodded. "It is the sky he will sleep beneath."

He placed a hand on Nebre's shoulder.

"As soon as the drips stop," he said, "we begin the walls."

The workers filed out quietly, leaving the chamber glowing gold in the lamplight. The ceiling was nearly dry. The walls waited below – blank, expectant, ready for the story of a king.

Nebre lingered a moment longer, staring upward. The sky was set. The earth would follow.

Chapter 15: The First Wall

The ceiling had dried to a steady gold by late afternoon. The last of the yellow drips had fallen onto the reed mats, leaving tiny flecks like scattered sunlight. Menna stood beneath the glow, watching the apprentices fan the air one final time.

When the ceiling no longer glistened, he placed his hand on the wall.

"Begin the earth."

The words carried through the chamber like a command from the mountain itself.

Two plasterers from the next rotation stepped forward, mixing a fresh bowl of gypsum. The sound was thick and wet – a rhythm Nebre was beginning to recognize. They pressed the plaster onto the north wall, smoothing it in long strokes.

Nebre watched the surface change from rough stone to a pale, living skin.

"Grandfather," he said quietly, "why this wall first?"

Menna did not answer immediately. He stepped back, studying the broad expanse of the north wall as though seeing it anew.

"This is the king's wall," he said at last. "The first he will face when he enters eternity. The wall of arrival. The wall of protection, the guardians."

Nebre's eyes widened. "And the guardians?"

Menna nodded. "Four of them. Isis, Nephthys, Selket, and Neith. They stand watch over the king's body and his spirit. They guard the four sons of Horus, and through them, the king's own organs. They are the first to greet him in the next world."

Nebre swallowed. "So they must be perfect."

"They must be true," Menna said. "Perfection is for the gods. Truth is for us."

The plasterers stepped aside. The scribes stepped in.

They climbed the scaffold, chalk cords looped over their shoulders. Nebre held a lamp beneath them, the glow catching the red dust on their fingers.

One scribe measured the wall with a knotted cord. The other snapped the first vertical line.

Nebre frowned. "What if the picture doesn't fit?"

Menna's answer was immediate.

"Then the scribe has failed. The wall must fit the story, and the story must fit the wall."

The scribes snapped horizontal lines next, forming a grid of squares. They checked the corners, adjusting the spacing with tiny shifts of the cord.

Nebre pointed. "Why stop the line there?"

"Because a king does not bend around a corner," Menna said. "Borders may wrap. Stories do not."

Behind them, the scribes ground pigment in shallow bowls. The sound was soft, like sand being sifted. The copper disks on their linen headbands caught the chamber lamp's glow, scattering warm light across the fresh plaster.

Nebre carried water to them, careful not to spill.

"Do they paint now?" he asked.

"When the grid is true," Menna said. "Not before."

The scribes finished their last line and stepped down. Menna inspected the grid with a practiced eye.

"Good. Bring the template."

The scribes moved to fetch the linen roll, but Menna did not follow. Instead, he lowered himself onto the reed mat beside the scaffold, the lamplight softening the lines of his face. Nebre hesitated, then sat beside him, setting down the water bowl.

For a moment, the chamber was quiet — only the faint whisper of palm fronds and the soft crackle of the lamp wick.

Menna reached beneath his sash and drew out a small carved lion.

Nebre's breath caught. He had seen it before — on his grandfather's table in the village, in the quiet hours when Menna worked alone — but never here, never in the tomb.

"My father carved that," Nebre whispered.

"Yes," Menna said. His thumb traced the worn curve of the lion's back. "He carved it for you."

Nebre looked up sharply. "For me?"

"He meant to give it to you on the day you became a painter. A gift from father to son. A beginning." Menna's voice softened. "He should be here. He should be standing beside us on this wall."

Nebre swallowed hard. "I wish he were."

Menna placed the lion in Nebre's hands.

"He is," he said. "And now you carry him. As he carried me. As I carry you."

Nebre held the lion as though it were alive, the wood warm from Menna's touch.

Menna rested a hand on his grandson's shoulder.

"You are no longer an apprentice," he said. "Today you join our line. Your father stood where you stand now, at your age, mixing my pigments. And now you will paint this wall with me — the two of us, and him beside us in spirit."

Nebre's eyes shone in the lamplight.

Menna rose slowly, steady and sure.

"Come," he said. "The king's guardian waits. And we will paint him together."

Chapter 16: The North Wall

By the time the next rotation entered the chamber, the first guardian's outline had dried to a soft, steady black. The chamber lamp glowed against the yellow ceiling, casting warm light across the fresh grid. The north wall — the king's wall — waited for its story.

Nebre stood near the scaffold, a bowl of clean water in one hand and the carved lion tucked safely inside his sash. He felt the shift in the room. The ceiling had been craft. This was something else. This was the beginning of the sacred.

Menna stepped forward, touching the wall lightly with his fingertips — the same gesture he had used when teaching Nebre's father.

"We continue," he said.

The plasterers moved first, smoothing the next section of wall. Their strokes were practiced, almost silent. The plaster shone wetly in the lamplight.

Nebre stepped closer than he ever had before, watching the texture, memorizing the sheen. Menna noticed and gave a small nod — the nod of a master to a painter, not to a boy.

The scribes climbed the scaffold, chalk cords ready. Nebre watched them measure the next grid, adjusting the spacing so the second figure would stand level with the first.

"Why do they measure again?" Nebre asked.

"Because no two walls are the same," Menna said. "Stone shifts. Corners lie. The grid must obey the wall, not the other way around."

The scribes snapped the vertical lines. Then the horizontals. The grid settled into place like a net catching light.

A painter unrolled the second template — another guardian, arms outstretched, posture mirroring the first.

Nebre leaned close. "Who is she?"

"Nephthys," Menna said. "Sister of Isis. Protector of the night. She stands beside her always."

Nebre studied the faint lines on the linen. "They look the same."

"They are not," Menna said. "Look at the hands. The tilt of the head. The way the feet stand. The gods are like people — each has a face."

The painters held the template to the grid. The scribes checked alignment. The rope man steadied the scaffold. The lamp tender trimmed the wick.

Nebre mixed a fresh bowl of black pigment, just as his father once had, and handed it to Menna without being asked.

The painter dipped his brush and traced the first line.

The second guardian woke from the wall.

As the painters stepped down to rest their hands, Menna reached into the small leather pouch tied at his waist. He drew out a bundle wrapped in linen — worn, stained, and tied with a simple cord.

Nebre recognized it instantly.

His father's brushes.

Menna held them for a moment, thumb brushing the frayed ends, then placed the bundle in Nebre's hands.

"These were his," Menna said. "He learned with them. He painted his first true line with them. And now they are yours."

Nebre's breath trembled. "Grandfather... I don't know if I'm ready."

"You are," Menna said. "You have practiced since you were small. You know the stroke. You know the weight. And you know the wall."

Nebre swallowed. "But this is a king's chamber."

Menna's voice softened. "Your father stood where you stand now, at your age. He mixed my pigments. He painted beside me. And now you will paint beside me too — with his brushes, and with him watching."

Nebre closed his fingers around the bundle, feeling the worn wood, the history, the lineage.

Menna nodded toward the wall.

"Come. The next guardian waits for your hand."

The rotation continued.

Plasterers. Scribes. Painters. Grinders. Lamp tenders. Carpenters. Apprentices with palm fronds.

Each team stepped into the footprints of the last, continuing the work as though they were the same hands.

The third guardian took shape — Selket, the scorpion goddess, her arms outstretched in protection. Nebre climbed the scaffold beside Menna, holding his father's brushes. Under Menna's steady guidance, he painted a small section of Selket's headdress — a single curve, but true.

Menna said nothing, but the pride in his eyes was unmistakable.

"Why her?" Nebre asked quietly.

"Because she guards the breath," Menna said. "She keeps poison from the king."

Nebre shivered, though the chamber was warm. His hand brushed the carved lion beneath his sash, grounding him.

The fourth guardian followed — Neith, ancient and stern, her presence filling the last section of the north wall. Her outline was taller, her posture straighter, her gaze fixed forward.

Nebre whispered, "She looks like she's watching us."

Menna nodded. "She watches everything. She is older than the kings."

The painters traced her final line. The scribes stepped back. The apprentices fanned the air to keep dust from settling.

The four guardians stood in a row, facing inward, their outlines dark and sure against the pale plaster.

Nebre felt it before he understood it.

The room had changed.

The ceiling had been craft. The grid had been craft. The first outline had been craft.

But four divine figures standing shoulder to shoulder — that was something else.

The chamber felt smaller. Quieter. Heavier.

Menna sensed it too. He stood in the center of the room, looking from one guardian to the next.

"This is the king's wall," he said softly. "The first he will see when he enters eternity."

Nebre swallowed. “Is it finished?”

“No,” Menna said. “This is only the beginning. The color comes next. The life.”

He placed a hand on Nebre’s shoulder – the same shoulder he had touched when giving him the lion.

“But the guardians are here now. They will watch over us as we work.”

Nebre nodded, feeling the weight of the lion against his chest, the weight of his father’s brushes in his hand, and the weight of the lineage he now carried.

The next team entered. The lamp tenders trimmed the wick. The plasterers prepared the next section of wall. The scribes checked their cords. The painters ground pigment. The apprentices fanned the air.

The chamber hummed with purpose.

The north wall glowed beneath the yellow ceiling, the four guardians standing watch – silent, patient, eternal.

Nebre looked up at them one last time before mixing the next bowl of pigment.

The king’s story had begun. And the walls were waking.

Chapter 17: The First Colors

The next morning, the chamber lamp burned steady and low, its flame trimmed to a fine point. The outlines of the four guardians stood dark and sure against the pale plaster, waiting. The room felt different now – not just sacred, but expectant.

Nebre stood beside Menna, holding his father's brushes in one hand and a bowl of clean water in the other. The carved lion rested inside his sash, warm against his chest.

Menna set a small wooden tray on the reed mat. On it lay four lumps of pigment:

yellow ochre

red ochre

soot black

powdered gypsum white

Nebre frowned slightly. "Only these?"

Menna smiled – the soft, knowing smile of a man who had waited years to give this lesson.

"For a king," he said, "these are enough."

He picked up the yellow ochre first, rolling it between his fingers.

"This," Menna said, "is the color of the sun. The color of Ra's first breath. The color of divine flesh."

Nebre leaned closer.

"Why not gold?" he asked.

Menna chuckled. "Gold is for the coffin, not the wall. Gold blinds the eye. Yellow guides it."

He placed the ochre in Nebre's palm.

"Every god you paint will wear this color. It tells the king he is among his own."

Menna lifted the red ochre next.

"This is the color of life," he said. "The color of blood, of strength, of the desert that protects us."

Nebre nodded. "And of men's skin."

"Yes," Menna said. "But not here. In a king's chamber, red is used sparingly. Too much life confuses the dead."

He tapped the red stone lightly.

"A line of red can wake a figure. Too much can drown it."

Menna picked up the soot black.

"This is the most important color of all," he said. "Black is the color of the fertile earth, the color of rebirth, the color of the night sky where the gods travel."

Nebre touched the pigment. It stained his fingertip instantly.

"And it is the line," Menna said. "The line that separates the living from the dead, the figure from the wall, the god from the stone."

He held Nebre's gaze.

"Your father learned this lesson first. You will learn it now."

Finally, Menna lifted the gypsum white.

"This is the color of breath," he said. "Of linen. Of purity. Of the first light before dawn."

Nebre nodded slowly. "For the eyes?"

"For the eyes," Menna said. "And for the places where the gods must shine."

He set the pigments down.

“These four colors are the bones of the world. With them, you can paint anything – if your hand is true.”

Nebre knelt beside him. “I thought the king would have more colors.”

Menna shook his head.

“In life, yes. In palaces, yes. But in death, the king needs only truth. Too many colors distract the spirit. Too much beauty blinds it.”

He placed a hand on Nebre’s shoulder.

“A king must see clearly on his journey. These colors guide him.”

Menna poured a thin stream of water into a shallow bowl. “Mix the yellow.”

Nebre ground the pigment with the wooden pestle, the motion familiar from years of practice on scraps of plaster and broken potsherds. But today felt different. Today the pigment mattered.

Menna watched him with quiet pride. “Your father mixed his first bowl at your age. He spilled half of it on my lap.”

Nebre smiled despite himself. “Did you scold him?”

“No,” Menna said. “I told him the gods would forgive him. And they did. They brought me you.”

When the pigment reached the right consistency – thick, smooth, and glowing – Menna dipped his finger into it and drew a small line on the rim of the bowl.

“Good,” he said. “Now bring it to the wall.”

Nebre carried the bowl carefully, climbing the scaffold beside Menna. The second guardian — Nephthys — waited, her outline steady and calm.

Menna placed a hand on Nebre's shoulder.

"Remember what I taught you," he said. "A line is a breath. A stroke is a heartbeat. And color is life."

Nebre nodded.

Menna handed him one of his father's brushes.

"Begin here," Menna said, pointing to the curve of Nephthys's arm. "A small place. A safe place. The gods will guide your hand."

Nebre dipped the brush into the yellow pigment. His hand trembled — not from fear, but from the weight of the moment.

He touched the brush to the wall.

The color spread in a smooth, golden arc.

Menna exhaled softly. "Good. Again."

Nebre painted another stroke. Then another. The guardian's arm began to glow with divine flesh.

Menna guided him gently, adjusting the angle of his wrist, the pressure of his fingers, the rhythm of his breathing.

"You see?" Menna murmured. "Your father is here. His hand is in yours."

Nebre swallowed hard. "I feel it."

They worked together — grandfather and grandson, master and painter, lineage and legacy — filling the guardian with life.

Below them, the chamber hummed with the sounds of the rotation:

plasterers mixing
scribes snapping lines

apprentices fanning the air

pigment grinders working in steady circles

But on the scaffold, time felt still.

When the section was complete, Menna stepped back.

"You have painted in a king's tomb," he said. "Your father would be proud."

Nebre looked at the glowing curve of Nephthys's arm, then at the brushes in his hand.

"So am I," he whispered.

Menna nodded once. "Come. The next color waits."

Chapter 18: The Last Figure

The chamber was quieter than usual.

Most of the scaffolding had been taken down. The baskets of plaster were nearly empty. The pigment grinders worked in slow, steady circles, as though they too felt the end approaching. Only one section of wall remained unfinished – a small figure near the western corner, a minor deity who would stand behind the king on his journey.

Nebre stood before it, his father's brushes in hand.

Menna watched him from a short distance, arms folded, the carved lion's absence from his sash noticed only by Nebre. It was tucked safely inside Nebre's own sash now, warm against his ribs.

"This one is yours," Menna said.

Nebre swallowed. "All of it?"

"All of it," Menna said. "Your first full figure. Your father painted his first at your age. Now you will paint yours."

Nebre stepped closer to the wall. The outline was already there – drawn by Menna the day before – but the figure was empty, waiting for life.

Waiting for him.

He dipped the brush into the yellow pigment he had mixed himself. The color glowed like morning light.

Menna's voice was soft behind him. "Remember what I taught you. A line is a breath. A stroke is a heartbeat. And color is life."

Nebre nodded and touched the brush to the wall.

The first stroke was smooth. Confident. True.

He filled the deity's arm, then the curve of the shoulder, then the long, elegant neck. The figure began to glow with divine flesh. Nebre's breath steadied. His hand found its rhythm.

He heard his father's voice in memory – not words, but the sound of him humming while he carved the lion.

Menna stepped closer, watching. "Good. Your hand is sure."

Nebre dipped into the red ochre next, adding the narrow band of the collar, the sacred mark on the wrist. Then the black – the line that defined the eye, the curve of the brow, the edge of the headdress.

The figure came alive under his hand.

When he stepped back, the deity stood complete – small, but perfect. A true painter's work.

Menna exhaled slowly. "Your father would have stood here today. But you stand in his place. And you honor him."

Nebre's throat tightened. "I wish he could see it."

"He does," Menna said. "He sees it in your hand."

They stood together in silence, looking at the figure glowing softly in the lamplight.

Behind them, the overseer Panehsy entered the chamber with two scribes. He inspected the walls with a practiced eye, nodding once.

"The work is nearly finished," he said. "The chamber will soon be cleaned. The scaffolds removed. The king's burial will begin."

Nebre felt the words like a stone in his chest.

The chamber would soon be sealed. The guardians would stand alone. The walls would belong to the king forever.

Menna placed a hand on Nebre's shoulder. "Come. Let us gather our tools."

Nebre hesitated.

"Grandfather... when the tomb is sealed... our work stays. But we leave. And no one will know we were here."

Menna nodded. "That is the way of our craft."

Nebre looked back at the figure he had painted – his first full figure, his father's brushes still warm in his hand.

"It doesn't feel right," he whispered. "We guided the king in life. Shouldn't we guide him in death?"

Menna studied him quietly.

Nebre touched the carved lion beneath his sash. "We could leave something. Something of us. Something of him."

Menna's eyes softened – not with surprise, but with recognition.

He had been thinking the same thing.

"Perhaps," Menna said, "the king would welcome such a gift."

Nebre nodded. "For him. For my father. For all of us."

Menna placed both hands on Nebre's shoulders.

“Then tonight,” he said, “we will gather what must be left behind.”

Nebre felt a shiver – not of fear, but of purpose.

His first figure was complete. His lineage was alive. And now, he would leave something of that lineage for the king to carry into eternity.

The chamber hummed softly around them, as though listening.

The tomb would soon close. But tonight, they would prepare their offering.

CHAPTER 19: THE OFFERING

The next morning, the tomb felt different.

Not quieter – the corridors still echoed with the scrape of wood, the thud of chests, the low chanting of men carrying shrines – but heavier, as though the air itself understood what was coming.

The burial chamber was no longer a place of work. It was becoming a place of rest.

Nebre and Menna stood just inside the doorway, watching as the last of the scaffolding was carried out. The walls glowed softly in the lamplight – the guardians, the king, the gods – all waiting for the final rites.

A team of cleaners entered next, dropping to their knees without a word. They moved slowly, reverently, inspecting every inch of the painted walls. Their linen cloths brushed the plaster with the gentleness of a blessing.

Nebre watched them work. "They clean the walls like they're touching a body."

"They are," Menna said. "The king's body. His eternal one."

The cleaners smoothed drips, polished edges, removed stray chalk marks. One paused before Nebre's figure – the small deity he had painted the day before – and nodded in approval before moving on.

Nebre felt a warmth rise in his chest.

The deity would stand here forever. His hand would remain on the wall long after he was dust.

A procession of men entered next, carrying the first pieces of the great gilded shrine. The chamber filled with the scent of cedar and resin as they maneuvered the massive panels into place. Nebre and Menna stepped back against the wall to give them room.

Piece by piece, the shrine rose — golden, towering, enclosing the space where the king would lie. The chamber grew smaller with every panel set into place.

Nebre whispered, "It feels like the room is closing around him."

Menna nodded. "That is the purpose. To protect him."

When the final panel was set, the high priest entered.

He wore a leopard skin over his shoulder, the mark of his office. His staff tapped softly against the stone as he approached the painted wall. He studied the guardians, the king, the gods — and finally, Nebre's small deity.

He placed his palm against the wall.

"True," he said. "The work is true."

Menna bowed his head. Nebre followed.

The priest turned to them. "You have served the king well. Your hands have honored him."

Nebre felt his throat tighten. Menna's eyes glistened.

The priest lifted his staff. "If you have an offering for the king's journey, present it now."

Nebre looked at Menna — surprised, relieved, grateful.

Menna stepped forward. "We do."

They had prepared it the night before:

the carved lion

the alabaster box

the small plates

one of Nebre's father's brushes

the copper disk

a small wooden container of ochre

the linen headband with their family emblem

a folded scrap of linen marked with their lineage sign

Menna held the bundle in both hands, wrapped in clean linen.

"This is a family offering," he said. "A guide for the king. A remembrance of those who served him."

The priest studied the bundle, then nodded.

"It is fitting."

Nebre exhaled softly.

The priest gestured toward the Antechamber. "Place it where the king will pass. Let it be known to him, but hidden from the world."

Menna and Nebre carried the bundle into the Antechamber.

The room was crowded with chests, beds, baskets, and boxes — a forest of objects waiting for eternity. The lamplight flickered across gold and wood and linen.

Nebre found a place near a tall basket woven of palm fiber, its lid tied with faded cord. Behind it was a narrow space, shadowed and still.

He knelt and placed the bundle gently behind the basket.

The carved lion faced outward, its small wooden eyes watching the room.

Menna rested a hand on Nebre's shoulder. "He will see it," he said. "And he will know."

Nebre nodded.

They stood in silence for a long moment, the weight of the offering settling around them like dust.

Then Menna spoke softly. "Come. Our part is done."

They stepped back into the burial chamber. The priest raised his staff, chanting the first words of the sealing rites. The shrine loomed golden and immense. The guardians watched from the walls.

Nebre looked once more at the figure he had painted – his first full figure, his father's brushes still warm in his hand.

He whispered a quiet farewell.

The tomb would soon close.

And their offering would remain.

Chapter 20: Harry Burton

The corridor outside the Antechamber echoed with hurried footsteps and the low murmur of voices. Lamps flickered against the limestone walls, throwing long shadows that swayed like reeds in a river current.

Howard Carter stood just inside the doorway, hands on his hips, surveying the crowded room with a mixture of exhaustion and exhilaration.

"Harry," he called over his shoulder, "no one will believe what we're about to reveal. Three thousand three hundred years untouched. It's... beyond anything."

Harry Burton, his camera slung over one shoulder, stepped into the Antechamber with two assistants carrying tripods and plate boxes.

Burton gave a thin smile. "Let's make sure the world sees it clearly, then."

Carter nodded, wiping dust from his brow. "Get a few quick plates of the shrine pieces before we need to go back up. Then take something of this room — just enough for the record. We'll come back later when we've more torches and a bit more air."

He coughed lightly. "It's getting difficult to breathe in here."

Burton nodded. "We'll be quick."

Carter stepped aside, giving the photographer room. "I'll fetch more lamps. Don't move anything unless you must."

He disappeared down the corridor, his footsteps fading.

Burton exhaled, adjusting the strap of his camera. "All right, lads. Let's get to it."

The Antechamber was a maze of objects — beds shaped like divine beasts, chests stacked like miniature houses, baskets, boxes, jars, and bundles. Dust motes drifted in the lamplight like tiny drifting stars.

Burton scanned the room. "Let's start with that corner. Good texture. Good contrast."

His assistant followed his gaze to a tall woven basket near the wall. In front of it sat a small carved lion, half in shadow, half in the warm spill of lamplight.

"Look at that," the assistant murmured. "Little toy lion?"

"Could be," Burton said. "Or a votive piece. Hard to say."

He knelt to adjust the tripod legs, angling the camera toward the basket. The lion's wooden face stared outward, steady and calm, exactly as Menna and Nebre had placed it.

The assistant reached toward the basket. "Should I move this a bit? It's crowding the frame."

"Careful," Burton said. "Don't knock over the lion."

"I see it."

"Leave it where it is. Natural is better."

The assistant stepped back, lifting the lamp higher. The flame flickered across the basket, the folded linen behind it, and the faint outline of an alabaster box just visible in the shadows.

Burton ducked under the dark cloth, adjusting the focus. The lion sharpened in the ground glass — a small, perfect detail in a room overflowing with history.

"Interesting little thing," he murmured. "Might make a good detail plate later."

He straightened, set the plate, and prepared the exposure.

"Hold the lamp steady."

The assistant steadied the flame.

Burton opened the shutter.

Light washed over the scene — over the basket, over the linen, over the hidden offering placed there by hands long turned to dust.

A moment of stillness.

Then the shutter closed.

"That's it," Burton said. "Next angle."

They moved on, leaving the lion exactly where it had been for more than three thousand years.

Watching. Waiting. Remembered only by the walls.

Chapter 21: Petal and Jerome

The winter sun hung low over the Nile, turning the river into a ribbon of hammered gold. Feluccas drifted lazily across the water, their sails catching the pale morning light. Luxor in 1922 was a place between worlds — ancient stone and modern dust, quiet villages and sudden bursts of excavation noise, diplomats and archaeologists sharing the same narrow streets.

Petal Whitcombe stepped off the small river launch, adjusting the strap of her leather camera satchel. She wore a linen blouse, a wide brimmed hat, and the unmistakable expression of someone who had spent her life chasing light.

Her husband, Jerome Whitcombe, followed behind her, offering a hand as she stepped onto the dock. He was tall, impeccably dressed despite the heat, and carried the calm, measured air of a British diplomat. But Petal noticed the faint strain around his eyes — the lingering fatigue he had been trying to hide since their last stop in Khartoum.

"Are you quite sure you're well enough for this?" she asked softly.

Jerome smiled. "My dear, I've survived worse than Egyptian winter air. Besides, you've been talking about Luxor since we left London. I wouldn't dare keep you from it."

They were in Egypt on a diplomatic circuit — a goodwill tour through British administered territories, meant to strengthen ties and assess local conditions. But for Petal, the journey had been something more: a chance to photograph landscapes she had only ever painted from memory and museum sketches.

And now, by sheer luck or fate, they had arrived in Luxor at the very moment the world was about to change.

A young man in a dusty shirt hurried toward them. “Mrs. Whitcombe? Mr. Whitcombe? The residence is ready for you. And Mr. Carter sends his apologies — he’s been called back to the tomb.”

Petal exchanged a glance with Jerome. “Howard Carter?”

“Yes, madam. He’s working with the photographer today. They’ve uncovered... well, something extraordinary.”

Jerome chuckled. “Petal, if you run now, you’ll leave me behind.”

She didn’t deny it.

They followed the young man through the winding streets to the diplomatic residence — a modest but comfortable building overlooking the river. As they approached, Petal noticed a cluster of crates stacked near the entrance, each marked with stenciled numbers and the seal of the Antiquities Service.

Inside, the air buzzed with excitement. Voices echoed down the hallway. Someone hurried past carrying a stack of glass photographic plates wrapped in linen.

Petal’s pulse quickened.

“Is Harry Burton here?” she asked.

The young man nodded. “Yes, madam. He’s set up a temporary darkroom in the rear courtyard. They’re bringing items from the tomb for cataloging.”

Jerome raised an eyebrow. “You’ll be impossible to keep away now.”

Petal squeezed his hand. “You knew that when you married me.”

They dropped their luggage in their room – a simple space with a carved wooden armoire, a writing desk, and a window overlooking the courtyard – and made their way outside.

The courtyard was a hive of activity.

Tripods leaned against the walls. Sheets of linen hung from ropes to diffuse the harsh sun. Assistants moved carefully between tables covered with artifacts wrapped in linen and straw. And in the center of it all stood Harry Burton, sleeves rolled up, adjusting the focus on his large wooden camera.

He looked up as Petal approached.

“Mrs. Whitcombe, isn’t it? I heard you were a photographer.”

“Of sorts,” she said. “Mostly landscapes. And the occasional diplomat.”

Jerome bowed theatrically. “A very occasional one.”

Burton grinned. “Well, if you’re willing, we could use another pair of careful hands. The objects are coming in faster than we can prepare them.”

Petal’s heart leapt. “I’d be honored.”

Jerome touched her arm. “Go on. I’ll rest a bit. The journey has caught up with me.”

She studied him — the pallor, the slight tremor — but he waved her off with a reassuring smile.

"I'll be fine. Just a short rest."

Petal nodded reluctantly and turned back to Burton.

"What can I do?"

Burton gestured to a long table covered in linen. "Help us unwrap and arrange the smaller items. Keep them in order, keep them clean, and keep them safe. Some of these pieces haven't seen light since before Moses."

Petal slipped into the rhythm easily — unwrapping, arranging, noting the textures and shapes, the way the light caught on gold or stone. She felt the same quiet reverence she had felt in museums as a girl, except now the objects were alive with dust and history.

A crate arrived, carried by two men. Burton glanced at the label.

"Antechamber. Basket 429B. Let's have a look."

Petal stepped forward, heart pounding.

The lid was pried open. Inside, wrapped in linen and straw, were small objects — humble, personal, unlike the grand shrines and chariots she had seen earlier.

She lifted the first piece.

A small carved wooden lion.

Its face was simple, earnest, almost childlike.

She smiled. "Oh, you're lovely."

Burton nodded. "Set it there. We'll photograph it with the others."

Petal reached for the next item — a small alabaster case, its lid slightly ajar, a thin line of dark resin clinging to the edge.

She felt a strange tug in her chest.

"Careful with that one," Burton said. "Looks delicate."

Petal placed it gently on the linen.

She didn't know it yet, but she was touching the past — Menna's hands, Nebre's hands — all in one small, unassuming box.

And the story was about to turn.

Chapter 22: The Darkroom Chaos

The courtyard darkroom was hotter than the desert outside.

Canvas sheets hung from ropes overhead, filtering the sun into a soft, amber glow. Tables were crowded with artifacts wrapped in linen, glass plates waiting to be exposed, brushes, cloths, and the ever present smell of chemicals drifting from the shaded corner where Harry Burton kept his trays.

Petal rolled up her sleeves and stepped into the rhythm of the room.

Assistants moved around her in a steady current – carrying crates, adjusting lamps, whispering instructions, arguing over catalog numbers. Every few minutes someone rushed in with a new object from the tomb, wrapped in straw and dust, as though the past itself were being delivered in armfuls.

Burton's voice cut through the noise. "Careful with that chest – it's older than half the gods."

Petal smiled. She liked him. He had the eye of an artist and the patience of a man who knew history could not be rushed.

A crate was set on the table beside her.

"Basket 429B," one of the assistants said. "Straight from the Antechamber."

Petal loosened the twine and folded back the linen.

Inside lay the small, humble objects she had glimpsed earlier — the ones that felt different from the gold and grandeur of the tomb.

She lifted the carved wooden lion first. Its face was simple, earnest, almost alive.

She set it gently on the linen.

Next came the linen headband, still faintly smelling of dust and resin. Then the wooden ochre container, its lid stained with pigment. Then the copper disk, dulled by centuries. Then the small carved plates, smooth and cool in her hands. Then the brush, its bristles stiff but intact.

And finally, the alabaster case.

Its lid sat slightly askew, a thin line of dark resin clinging to the edge like a memory.

Petal touched it with the same reverence she had once given her father's old camera.

"Beautiful," she whispered.

Burton approached, wiping his hands on a cloth. "Let's photograph these together. They look like a set."

"A personal set," Petal said. "Not royal."

Burton nodded. "Yes. Someone's tools. Someone's life."

Before they could begin, a shout echoed from the far end of the courtyard.

"Harry! Carter needs you — now! The shrine panel is slipping!"

Burton swore under his breath. "Of all the times..."

He turned to Petal. "Don't move anything. I'll be right back."

He hurried off, assistants trailing behind him.

Petal remained at the table, alone for the first time since she had arrived. She studied the objects — the lion, the plates, the brush — feeling a strange, quiet pull in her chest.

These weren't treasures. They were memories.

She reached for her notebook to sketch the arrangement, but before she could begin, another assistant rushed in — a young man with a lamp in one hand and a coil of cable in the other.

"Sorry, miss — need to clear this table. They want the space for the shrine plates."

Petal opened her mouth to protest, but he was already moving.

He gathered the objects quickly — too quickly — scooping them into the alabaster case as though tidying a child's toys. The lion went in first, then the plates, then the brush, then the headband, then the copper disk, then the ochre container.

"Wait—" Petal began.

But he didn't hear her.

He pressed the lid onto the case.

The resin — warmed by the sun, softened by time — sealed.

A soft, sticky click.

The assistant wiped his hands. "There. All tidy."

Petal stared at the alabaster case.

It looked like a single, solid block now — seamless, innocent, mute.

"Where should I put it?" the assistant asked.

"Just... set it aside," Petal said quietly.

He placed it on a nearby shelf, among dozens of other objects waiting to be cataloged.

Petal watched him go.

She felt a strange ache in her chest – as though something important had just slipped through her fingers, though she couldn't have said why.

She reached for the case, hesitated, then let her hand fall.

Burton's voice echoed from the courtyard. "Petal! We need you for the lighting!"

She turned away from the shelf and hurried toward the commotion.

Behind her, the alabaster case sat in the warm Egyptian light, its contents sealed again after more than three thousand years.

Waiting for the next pair of hands.

Chapter 23: The Anniversary Gift

Jerome Whitcombe had never been a man to wander without purpose. Diplomats rarely were. But that afternoon, as the sun dipped behind the western cliffs and the courtyard darkroom buzzed with frantic activity, he found himself drifting toward the linen draped tables without quite knowing why.

He had woken that morning with a fever behind his eyes and a heaviness in his limbs. Petal had noticed, of course — she always noticed — but he had brushed it off with a smile and a promise to rest.

He had rested. But the fever had not.

Now, as he walked past the open doorway of the darkroom, something caught his eye.

A small alabaster case sat on a shelf, half in shadow, half in the warm glow of a lantern. It was simple, elegant, unassuming — the kind of object easily overlooked among the gilded shrines and jeweled collars.

But Jerome stopped.

There was something about it — the smoothness of the stone, the faint sheen of resin along the lid, the quiet dignity of its shape.

He stepped closer.

A young lighting technician hurried past him, carrying a coil of cable. "Careful, sir — mind the plates."

Jerome nodded absently, his gaze fixed on the alabaster case.

Petal would love this.

She loved objects with stories. She loved things that had been touched by time. She loved the quiet poetry of the past.

And tomorrow was their tenth anniversary.

He reached out and lifted the case. It was heavier than he expected – solid, cool, comforting in his hands.

He turned it over gently. No markings. No catalog number. No indication that anyone had claimed it yet.

Just a small, perfect box.

A gift.

He slipped it under his arm and made his way back to their room.

The diplomatic residence was quiet in the late afternoon. The Nile breeze drifted through the open windows, carrying the scent of river water and distant cooking fires. Jerome closed the door behind him and set the alabaster case on the writing desk.

He sat for a moment, catching his breath. The fever pulsed behind his eyes again, sharper this time. He pressed a hand to his temple, waited for the wave to pass, then reached for a sheet of stationery.

His handwriting wavered slightly, but the words came easily.

My beloved Petal, For our tenth year together – a small piece of history for the woman who has given me a lifetime of light. Yours always, Jerome

He folded the note and tucked it beneath the alabaster case.

Then he opened the armoire — the same carved wooden one that they brought from England and placed the case and the note at the very back, behind a stack of neatly folded shawls.

Safe. Hidden. Waiting for morning.

He closed the doors gently.

A sudden chill ran through him. He steadied himself against the armoire, breathing slowly until the dizziness passed.

He should lie down. Just for a moment.

He made it to the bed, sat heavily, and pressed a hand to his chest.

The fever surged.

The room tilted.

He called Petal's name — softly, almost apologetically — but she was still in the courtyard, helping Burton with the shrine plates.

By the time she returned, the doctor had already been summoned.

By nightfall, Jerome Whitcombe was in the small Luxor hospital, his condition worsening by the hour.

By dawn, he was gone.

Chapter 24: The Journey Home

The morning after Jerome's death was a blur of voices, footsteps, and the soft rustle of linen. Petal moved through it as though underwater, her senses dulled, her breath shallow, her hands trembling whenever she reached for something that had belonged to him.

The diplomatic residence felt suddenly enormous — every room echoing with absence.

She returned to their bedroom to gather his things. The sunlight through the shutters fell in thin, pale stripes across the floor. His coat lay neatly folded on the chair. His hat rested on the desk. His shoes were placed side by side, as though waiting for him to return.

Petal opened the armoire.

The shawls shifted slightly, and something pale caught her eye.

The alabaster case.

And beneath it, the folded note.

Her breath caught.

She lifted the case with both hands, holding it as though it might break. Then she unfolded the note.

My beloved Petal...

Her vision blurred. She pressed the paper to her lips, then to her heart, her shoulders shaking with silent sobs.

This was his last act. His last thought. His last gift.

She sank to the floor, the case in her lap, the note clutched in her hand.

A soft knock sounded at the door. The doctor stepped inside, his expression gentle.

"Mrs. Whitcombe... I'm afraid I have more news."

She looked up, eyes red, breath unsteady.

"You are expecting a child," he said softly. "A few weeks along, I believe."

Petal closed her eyes.

A child. Jerome's child. A life beginning as his ended.

She placed a hand on her abdomen, feeling a warmth spread through her grief – not easing it, but giving it shape.

"This," she whispered to the unborn child, "is your father's gift to us."

Arrangements were made quickly.

The British Consulate insisted on handling the transport of Jerome's body. A simple wooden coffin was prepared, lined with linen. Petal stood beside it as the attendants worked, her hand resting on the alabaster case.

She could not bear to leave it behind. She could not bear to carry it openly. She could not bear the thought of customs officials prying it open.

She looked at the coffin.

At Jerome's still, peaceful face.

At the space between his calves and above his ankles – a narrow, secure place beneath the linen.

She made her decision.

When the attendants stepped away, she knelt beside the coffin and gently slid the alabaster case into the space between his legs, tucking it beneath the linen folds.

Safe. Hidden. Protected.

A final journey together.

She pressed her forehead to the wood. "I'll bring you home," she whispered.

The voyage back to England was long and quiet.

Petal spent most of it in her cabin, sketching the Nile from memory, tracing the curve of the lion's face in her mind, holding Jerome's note until the ink smudged at the edges.

She felt the child growing inside her — a small flutter, a promise.

When the ship finally docked in Southampton, the undertaker met her with a solemn bow.

"We'll prepare your husband for burial, Mrs. Whitcombe. You may rest."

She nodded, exhausted.

Hours later, the undertaker returned, carrying a small wrapped bundle.

"This was found in the coffin," he said. "We thought it must belong to you."

Petal's breath caught.

The alabaster case.

Still sealed. Still whole. Still carrying the weight of three thousand years — and the weight of her husband's last love.

"Thank you," she whispered.

She held the case to her chest as though it were a heartbeat.

That night, in the quiet of her childhood home, she placed the alabaster case in her small leather travel suitcase covered in travel stickers— the one she had carried across Africa, the one that held her camera equipment safe and secure.

She closed the suitcase gently.

The case would remain there for decades — untouched, unopened, sacred.

A memory. A mystery. A lineage waiting to be found.

Chapter 25: The Armoire

The armoire had traveled farther than most people ever would.

It had been shipped from England in 1920, part of the Whitcombes' personal furnishings for their long diplomatic posting through Africa. Petal insisted on bringing it – a carved oak piece with brass hinges and a deep bottom drawer that smelled faintly of lavender. It was familiar, sturdy, and large enough to hold her camera equipment and Jerome's neatly folded clothes.

When they reached Luxor in 1922, the armoire was carried into their room at the diplomatic residence, its weight creaking against the tiled floor. Petal placed her small leather suitcase in the bottom drawer – the same suitcase she had carried across Africa, its sides covered in travel stickers from Cairo, Khartoum, and Port Said.

And after Jerome's death, when she returned to England, the armoire returned with her.

So did the suitcase.

And inside the suitcase, wrapped in soft cloth, lay the alabaster case – sealed, silent, untouched.

Petal never opened it.

She couldn't. The case had become a vessel of memory, a final gesture of love, a bridge between the life she had lost and the life growing inside her. She placed the suitcase back into the bottom drawer of the armoire, slid it shut, and locked it with the small brass key.

She kept the key on a ribbon in her jewelry box.

For a time.

Years passed.

Amanda grew — first crawling across the bedroom floor, then toddling toward the armoire, fascinated by the brass handles. Petal would gently redirect her.

"That drawer stays closed," she would say softly. "It holds something precious."

Amanda accepted this without question. Children understand reverence instinctively.

When Amanda was old enough to have a room of her own, Petal moved the armoire into it. Not because Amanda needed it — but because Petal wanted the suitcase, and the alabaster case inside it, to remain close to her daughter's life.

During one of the moves — from London to the countryside — the armoire's bottom drawer handle snapped clean off. The brass key went missing somewhere between houses. The drawer stuck, swollen slightly from damp, refusing to open without force.

Petal didn't force it.

"One day, I'll have it repaired." She whispered.

But one day never came.

When Amanda married, Petal passed the armoire to her.

"It holds our family's story," she said. "Keep it safe."

Amanda placed it in her new home, the bottom drawer still stuck, the handle missing. She never tried to open it. She never needed to. She simply dusted the armoire, polished the brass hinges, and kept it exactly as her mother had given it.

More years passed.

Amanda had a daughter – Cherry – who grew up hearing stories of Egypt, of photography, of a diplomat father she had never met. Cherry loved the armoire, loved the carved patterns along its doors, loved the idea that it had crossed deserts and oceans.

When Amanda grew older, she passed the armoire to Cherry.

"This belonged to your grandmother," she said. "And her mother before her. Keep it safe."

Cherry placed the armoire in her own home – a different house, a different decade, but the same carved wood, the same brass hinges, the same stubborn bottom drawer. She never opened it. She never tried.

The alabaster case slept inside the suitcase. The suitcase slept inside the drawer. The drawer slept inside the armoire. The armoire slept inside the family.

Waiting.

And then came Abagail.

Cherry's daughter. Amanda's granddaughter. Petal's great granddaughter.

A woman who loved stories, who loved old things, who loved the quiet mystery of objects that carried more than they revealed.

When Cherry passed the armoire to her, Abagail ran her fingers over the carved wood, tracing the patterns worn smooth by three generations of hands.

"This was your great grandmother's," Cherry said. "And her mother's. And her mother's. Keep it safe."

Abagail placed the armoire in her attic — too heavy for the bedroom, too sentimental to discard, too damaged to use. The bottom drawer was still stuck. The handle still missing. The key still lost.

She meant to repair it.

One day.

But life filled the years, and the armoire remained in the attic, its drawer sealed by time and memory.

Inside it, the suitcase waited. Inside the suitcase, the alabaster case waited. Inside the alabaster case, the offering waited.

All of it untouched since 1922.

All of it waiting for caring hands.

Chapter 26: The Drawer Revealed

The attic was colder than Abagail remembered. She stood before the armoire, the bottom drawer still stuck, the handle missing, the key lost to time. She had meant to repair it for years, but life had always intervened.

Today, though, she was determined.

She pressed her hands against the drawer, feeling the wood shift beneath her touch. She tried gently, then firmly, then with a careful twist. The drawer refused to move.

She knelt, peering into the gap where the drawer met the frame. The seam was wider now, the wood swollen and cracked. She pressed harder, feeling the back of the armoire shift.

A sudden creak echoed through the attic. The entire back panel of the armoire slid loose, revealing a hidden cavity behind the drawer.

Abagail's breath caught.

She reached inside, her fingers brushing against something solid–leather, cracked and familiar. The suitcase.

She pulled it free, surprised by its weight. Something inside shifted–a muted, dense thud against the lining. Not clothes. Not papers. Something older.

She carried it downstairs, her heart pounding.

Emily was in the kitchen, sorting through a stack of envelopes. She looked up when Abagail entered, her expression softening in that way it always did when her daughter appeared with something unexpected.

Abagail set the suitcase on the table. "The armoire's back came loose. The drawer finally gave way."

Emily came closer. Her breath caught.

She rested her fingers on the lid, the way one might touch a sleeping animal.

The stickers. The leather. The initials.

"I haven't seen this since I was a child," she said quietly. "I thought it was lost."

She ran her fingers over the stickers, tracing the edges of Luxor Winter Palace as if the name might shift under her touch. She didn't say anything more. She didn't need to.

The suitcase looked out of place on the kitchen table—too old, too heavy with its own history. Emily tried one of the locks. It refused. The metal had seized long ago.

"No key?" she asked.

Abagail shook her head.

Emily studied the lock again. The metal was pitted, the mechanism stiff. She pressed her thumb against it, feeling for any give.

Nothing.

She sat down, the suitcase in front of her, and let out a slow breath.

"It's strange," she said. "Your grandmother kept everything in order. But this... she never mentioned it."

Abagail pulled out a chair and sat beside her. "Maybe she forgot about it."

Emily shook her head. "Cherry didn't forget things. Not things like this."

They sat in silence for a moment, the suitcase between them like a question neither of them knew how to ask.

Emily reached for the straps. The leather cracked softly under her touch. She eased one free, then the other.

The locks still refused.

Abagail leaned closer. "Do you want me to get a screwdriver?"

"No," Emily said. "Let's not force it."

She turned the suitcase slightly, examining the hinges, the seams, the way the leather had pulled away from the frame in places. Then she noticed a small tear near the back corner, just wide enough to slip a finger through.

She pressed gently. The lining shifted.

"Here," she murmured.

Together, they worked the lining loose, peeling it back just enough to reach inside. Emily's fingers brushed something smooth, cool, and solid.

She drew it out slowly.

A small alabaster box, wrapped in linen that had yellowed with age.

Abagail stared. "What is that?"

Emily didn't answer. She set the box on the table, her hands steady but her breath not quite.

The linen was soft, worn thin in places. She unwrapped it carefully, revealing the box beneath—

pale, translucent, the surface etched with faint scratches that caught the light.

The lid was slightly askew.

Emily touched it with the back of her finger, as if testing whether it was real.

"This wasn't my mother's," she said quietly. "Or Cherry's. This is older."

"How old?" Abagail asked.

Emily didn't look away from the box. "Old enough," she said. "Older than any ancestor I've ever heard of."

Chapter 27: The Unveiling

The kitchen was quiet, the kind of quiet that feels like a held breath. Afternoon light slanted across the table, warming the old leather suitcase and the small alabaster box that had slept inside it for more than a century.

Emily rested her fingertips on the lid of the box, not opening it yet. She simply held it, feeling the coolness of the stone, the faint unevenness of the resin seal, the weight of something that had been carried farther than she could comprehend.

Abagail watched her mother's face. There was something in Emily's expression she had never seen before — not fear, not awe, but recognition.

As though she had been waiting for this moment without knowing it.

Emily drew a slow breath and lifted the lid.

The resin cracked softly — a sound like a whisper escaping after too many years.

Inside, wrapped in linen that had yellowed to the color of old sunlight, lay the first object.

Emily lifted it gently.

A small carved lion, its wooden face worn smooth by hands long gone.

Abagail leaned closer. "It's... beautiful."

Emily nodded. "Someone loved this. You can feel it."

She set the lion on the linen cloth she had spread across the table — the same cloth that had once wrapped the box, the same cloth Petal had touched, the same cloth that had traveled across deserts and oceans.

Next came a folded linen headband, faintly smelling of dust and resin. Emily unfolded it slowly, revealing the faded lotus and feather stitched along the edge.

"A family mark," she murmured. "Or a workshop mark. Someone wore this with pride."

Abagail touched the embroidery with one finger. "Someone's identity."

Emily smiled softly. "Someone's belonging."

She placed the headband beside the lion.

Then she lifted a small wooden ochre container, its lid stained with pigment. The red dust clung to the grain of the wood, as though refusing to let go of the hand that last used it.

"A painter's pigment," Emily whispered. "Still here. Still red."

Abagail felt a shiver. "It survived."

Emily nodded. "Because someone cared enough to keep it."

Next came a thin copper disk, dulled by centuries. Emily held it up to the light, and the afternoon sun caught the metal, scattering a warm glow across the table.

Abagail inhaled sharply. "That's how they painted in the dark."

Emily nodded. "A reflector. A helper. A companion to the lamp."

She set it down gently.

Then she lifted a bundle of small carved plates, each etched with symbols — lotus, feather, square, dot, pairs, trios, patterns that felt like a language just beyond reach.

Abagail traced one with her thumb. “Instructions? A code? A lineage?”

Emily smiled. “A message. Not in words — in memory.”

She placed the plates beside the others.

Next came a brush, its bristles stiff but intact, the handle worn smooth by years of use.

Emily held it with both hands, as though greeting an old friend.

“This,” she said softly, “belonged to someone who painted with love. You can feel the hand in it.”

Abagail swallowed. “It’s like touching them.”

Emily nodded. “Exactly.”

Finally, Emily reached into the suitcase and lifted a small alabaster lamp, its interior stained with ancient residue.

She turned it in the light. “This lamp lit their work. This lamp lit their world.”

Abagail whispered, “And now it lights ours.”

Emily set the lamp beside the brush.

The table was full now — a painter’s life laid out like a quiet resurrection.

The lion. The headband. The ochre. The copper disk. The plates. The brush. The lamp.

A family. A workshop. A lineage. A memory.

Emily stepped back, her breath unsteady.

“These aren’t treasures,” she said. “They’re... someone’s life. Someone’s hands. Someone’s love.”

Abagail nodded, her eyes shining. "And someone carried them forward."

Emily looked at her daughter — really looked at her.

"Not someone," she said softly. "Many someones."

She touched the lion.

"Nebre."

She touched the brush.

"Menna."

She touched the suitcase.

"Petal."

She touched the note.

"Jerome."

She touched the armoire keyhole.

"Amanda."

She touched her own chest.

"Cherry."

Then she took Abagail's hand.

"And now us."

The afternoon light shifted, catching the copper disk again. A warm glow spread across the table — soft, golden, familiar.

A quiet echo of the past, alive in the present.

Emily squeezed Abagail's hand.

"We keep them safe," she said. "We remember. And we carry their story forward."

Abagail nodded.

Because now she understood:

The offering had survived not by accident, but by care.

By hands that loved. By hands that grieved. By hands that remembered. By hands that carried.

Across centuries. Across continents. Across lives.

And now, finally, the offering had reached the hands it was waiting for.

Chapter 28: The Plates of Memory

The alabaster box lay open on the table, its contents arranged in a quiet constellation of memory. But Emily wasn't looking at the artifacts anymore.

She was staring at the bottom of the suitcase.

"Something's under the lining," she murmured.

Abagail leaned closer. "Another compartment?"

Emily slipped her fingers beneath the torn edge of the fabric and lifted it gently. A thin stack of glass photograph plates slid into view, wrapped in tissue so fragile it crumbled at her touch.

Her breath caught.

"These are... old. Very old."

She lifted the first plate to the light.

A ship. London docks.

1920.

Jerome and Petal stood on the gangway, smiling in the pale English sun. Petal wore her travel hat, the same one Emily remembered from a faded portrait. Petal held a leather suitcase — this suitcase — the initials still visible on the clasp.

Abagail exhaled softly. "They look so young."

Emily nodded. "They were."

She set the plate down and lifted the next.

A Nile boat. Petal leaning against the railing, sketchbook in hand. Jerome beside her, pointing toward the western cliffs. Behind them, the river shimmered like hammered gold.

Abagail smiled. "They look like they belong there."

Emily's voice softened. "My mother always said Petal felt at home in Egypt."

She lifted the third plate.

A room overlooking the Nile — their room at the diplomatic residence. The window open. Curtains stirring. Petal's camera on the table. Jerome's coat on the chair.

And in the corner, half in shadow, unmistakable:

the same armoire now sitting in their attic.

Abagail gasped. "That's... ours."

Emily nodded slowly. "It traveled with them. Just like the suitcase."

She lifted another plate.

The courtyard. Assistants moving in a blur. Burton adjusting his camera. Carter in the background, sleeves rolled up.

And on a basket near the edge of the frame — almost an afterthought — the carved lion and the alabaster case.

Abagail whispered, "There they are."

Emily's throat tightened. "Petal saw them. She touched them. She photographed them."

She lifted the final plate.

The light room table. Howard Burton leaning over a set of artifacts. The copper disk. The brush. The headband. The ochre container. The carved plates.

And there — just off to the side, as though waiting patiently —

the lion and the alabaster case again.

Abagail stared at the image, her eyes shining. "It's like they were following her."

Emily shook her head gently. "No. She was following them."

They laid the plates out beside the artifacts, the past and present touching at the edges.

Emily rested her hand on the lion. "These weren't just objects. They were someone's tools. Someone's life. And Petal... she knew. She felt it."

Abagail nodded. "She carried them because she cared."

Emily looked at her daughter — really looked at her.

"And now we carry them."

The afternoon light shifted, catching the edge of the photograph plates. The lion's shadow stretched across the table. The copper disk glowed softly. The armoire upstairs creaked, as though remembering.

Emily exhaled.

"It's all connected," she said. "Every caring hand. Every choice. Every moment."

Abagail took her mother's hand.

Emily looked at the artifacts again — the lion, the brush, the lamp, the plates — and her voice dropped to a reverent whisper.

"These objects have been in our family for a century."

She touched the photograph of Petal, her fingers trembling.

"These objects were meant to be remembered."

Then she closed her hand around Abagail's, steady and sure. "We are the next caring hands."

Chapter 29: The Stillness

Evening settled slowly over the house, softening the edges of the kitchen and turning the artifacts on the table into silhouettes. Emily hadn't moved for several minutes. She sat with her hands folded loosely in her lap, her gaze drifting between the lion, the brush, the lamp, the plates, the suitcase.

Abagail watched her mother, sensing the shift — not fear, not confusion, but a kind of quiet reverence.

Emily finally spoke.

"It's strange," she said softly. "We know so little. And yet... I feel like I know them."

Abagail nodded. "I do too."

Emily reached for one of the carved plates — the one with the lotus and the feather. She traced the symbols with her thumb, not trying to decipher them, only feeling the grooves worn by another hand long ago.

"I don't know what these mean," she said. "And I don't think we're meant to."

Abagail leaned closer. "Do you think they're instructions?"

"Maybe," Emily said. "Or a record. Or a memory. Or something sacred. But whatever they were... they mattered to someone."

She set the plate down gently.

Abagail picked up the brush. The bristles were stiff, the handle smooth from years of use. She held it the way a painter might, testing its balance, imagining the hand that once guided it.

"Someone used this every day," she whispered. "Someone who cared about their work."

Emily smiled. "Someone who cared enough to keep it safe."

They sat in silence for a moment, the weight of the objects settling around them like a soft blanket.

Abagail looked at the lion. "Do you think it belonged to a child?"

Emily shook her head slowly. "I don't know. But it was loved. You can feel it."

She lifted the copper disk, turning it so the last of the daylight caught its edge. A warm glow flickered across the table – a small echo of the ancient light it once reflected.

Abagail watched the glow fade. "We'll never know the whole story, will we?"

Emily's expression softened. "No. And that's all right."

She looked at the artifacts again – the lion, the plates, the brush, the lamp – and her voice grew quiet, almost reverent.

"Some stories survive in full," she said. "Some survive in pieces. And some survive only because someone cared enough to carry them forward."

Abagail nodded, her eyes shining. "Like Petal."

"And Jerome," Emily added. "And Amanda. And Cherry."

She reached across the table and took Abagail's hand.

"And now us."

The room grew still. The last light slipped away. The artifacts rested in the soft glow of the kitchen lamp, no longer relics, no longer mysteries — simply objects waiting for the next caring hands.

Emily exhaled, a breath that felt like acceptance.

"These objects have been in our family for a century."

She touched the photograph of Petal, her fingers trembling just slightly.

"These objects were meant to be remembered."

Then she closed her hand around Abagail's, steady and sure.

"We are the next caring hands."

And in that moment, the story — the real story — settled quietly into their keeping.

Author's Note

This novella began with a simple question: *What survives?*

Not the names. Not the records. Not the full truth.

What survives are the fragments — objects carried forward by people who never knew their origins, stories preserved by accident and affection, and the quiet persistence of memory across generations.

Emily and Abagail do not know the full story behind what they inherit. They aren't meant to. Their role is not to solve the past, but to care for what remains of it.

The reader becomes the final keeper of the truth — the only one who sees the ancient world, the widow's grief, and the lineage that unknowingly protected a forgotten offering.

Some stories survive in full. Some survive in pieces. And some survive only because someone cared enough to carry them forward.

Thank you for carrying this one.

— David Ashe

David Ashe Bio

David Ashe believes stories are bridges — between science and philosophy, between imagination and memory. He is a speculative fiction author and watercolor artist whose work explores the intricate balance between humanity's resilience, cosmic forces, and philosophical inquiry.

As the creator of the *Tutankhamun novella and The Code of Evolution* saga, David crafts immersive narratives that blend cutting-edge technology, ancient wisdom, and themes of renewal. His storytelling is rich with emotion, thought - provoking tension, and characters who wrestle with the forces shaping their destinies — all while remaining clean and accessible for readers of any age.

Beyond writing, David's artistic vision extends into watercolor painting, where he captures ethereal landscapes and human depth in delicate, fluid strokes. His original works, featured on Amazon Handmade and recognized by his county's arts commission, reflect the same philosophical depth and craftsmanship found in his novels.

Whether through ink or brush, David's creative works resonate with themes of transformation, exploration, and the enduring power of human ingenuity — welcoming readers of all backgrounds into a world where science and philosophy intertwine.

The *Code of Evolution* saga is a five book journey through worlds on the brink of collapse, where cyber warfare, cosmic biotech, and ancient resonance intertwine. Beginning with *Code of Evolution*, the series follows Mara and her allies as they uncover a living archive of glyphs and mysteries that hold the key to humanity's survival. Each volume expands the scope — from shattered cities to reborn civilizations — blending high-stakes adventure with visionary themes of renewal, unity, and the transformative power of the human spirit. Together, the saga forms a sweeping chronicle of evolution itself, charting not only the survival of a species but the awakening of something greater.

Other Novels by David Ashe

The *Code of Evolution* Carathis Saga continues beyond this first volume, carrying readers deeper into a living archive of resonance, glyphs, and cosmic biotech. Across five books, the series traces humanity's struggle to survive collapse, rediscover unity, and awaken to a greater destiny. Each installment expands the scope — from fractured cities to reborn civilizations — weaving high-stakes adventure with visionary themes of renewal and transformation. This is only the beginning of a journey that will redefine what it means to evolve.

The Carathis Saga
A Completed Five Book Saga
Book One — Code of Evolution
"Every beginning is a braid of endings unseen."
— The First Memory
Book Two — Code of Evolution: Ascension
"To rise is to remember what was buried."
— The Keepers of the Thread
Book Three — Code of Evolution: Return to Gaia
"The world returns, but never as it was."
— Fragment of the Lost Chronicle
Book Four — Code of Evolution: Echo Gaia
"Carathis is not found. It is remembered."
— The Carathis Saga
Book Five — Code of Evolution:
Keystone Conduit
"The braid is sealed, yet its echo endures."
— Echoes of the Conduit Chronicles

www.ingramcontent.com/pod-product-compliance
Lightning Source LLC
LaVergne TN
LVHW090958080826
845145LV00003B/1052

* 9 7 8 1 9 3 7 7 7 4 0 8 0 *